LeFroy's Castle

By JP Cline

Introduction

I started writing this story back in 2014, after a trip to Ireland, where I exhibited my paintings. One evening I went to a pub in Howth, it was very cold out and I felt like I was a character in a Gothic novel, in the sense that it was cold, dark and gloomy and I was off to a big adventure. On that trip I met the most interesting people, for example, someone who works in a castle. I actually ended up having breakfast in a castle once. Coming from tropical Mexico where we haven't got that many castles, I felt a sort of "wow" moment where I thought about how in my country nobody has breakfast in castles and here in Ireland, since you have far more castles than we do in Mexico, chances of being invited to see one are greater than one's chances in Mexico.

Every castle on earth is believed to be haunted and I decided to write a short novel about a haunted castle. I have a big imagination and I think about ghosts, goblins, monsters, etc when I am certain places, such as castles, thick forests and so on. I also make up stories about where I am, I imagine the adventures of a lunatic or a mad scientist, or in this case a haunted castle.

I have a theme in my novel about dreams. There is a room in the house where it is believed that anybody that sleeps in it will have a dream where they see their death. I have always been interested in dreams and have often wondered "what if you could see the future in a dream?" That thought is what inspired me to write about the power of dreams. We all love dreams, I suppose, some of which we want to come true, others we wish wouldn't. In this case the characters, as I mentioned before, in a dream they see how they die, they cannot do anything about it but just the same, a spirit within the castle shows them the moment they die.

As for the setting, Howth means a lot to me. I love visiting Howth. I have many friends there. Unlike Howth which has one castle on the top of a hill, Clongriffin never once had a castle, in so far as I know. However I had visited a few castles in 2014, when I started writing this story and I imagined one. I called it Clongriffin Castle, taking the name from what is now a suburb of Dublin, but was mostly fields in the XIX century.

I hope you enjoy reading the story as much as I enjoyed writing it. The last thing I have to say about it, is, I am an artist. I paint and that is how I went to Ireland, to have my art shown in Dublin. That's where I got the idea for my story. Anyway, in art you tell a fraction of a story, but you can not tell an entire story. For example, if you paint a boat in the sunset, you don't tell people where the boat came from and where it is headed, much less who is in it and what they are up to inside the boat. So, you just tell people that there is a boat in the sunset. I did the same thing with my story. I give you an image of something that happened, an anecdote as it were, but I do not write volumes and volumes about who everyone was and where they came from and where they are headed. Because this is a written painting in the sense that you get a part of a story, which gives you an idea of what happened, and you decide in your mind what the story was before and what happened after. Like you do when you observe a painting. The idea of my story is for you to dream. It is a fantasy. That is why I kept it short but interesting. Dear reader, feel free to decide for yourself who the characters were before the story and what happened to them afterwards. I am only painting a picture of a short period in their life. It is up to you to dream about what happened to them before and after these events.

Please enjoy by story and have fun reading it.

Thanks so much, JP Cline

Chapter 1

It was a very cold winter in Ireland, then. Colder than it had been in a while. The north wind was so strong that one could imagine a herd of Polar Bears walking through the middle of Dublin. Polar Bears outside Christ Church Cathedral, and Polar Bears near the Liffey. Polar Bears on the Ha'Penny Bridge and Polar Bears as far as the coast. It was so tremendously cold out that night that very few people dared go out, for fear of being turned into an icicle.

Heath Rochester, a man in his thirty's had just arrived from England that night. He made it to a fishing village called Howth, hoping to find food, and a place to stay for the night, and keep warm. As he walked along Howth Harbour, in his dark coat, his hair blowing in the wind, and his hand in his pockets to keep warm, he saw a light on in a pub. Our friend, Heath, could not have been more pleased to see the pub for the cold was so tremendously bitter: He was dying for some warm pub food and a drink. Heath had also been walking for some time. You see he had set sail from England in order to seek adventure. He was an artist and had been told that Howth is a village that is very much worth painting.

"Pardon me, sir, do you serve food here?" Heath Rochester asked a man who worked in the public house as he walked in the place.

'Yea, we have, I can get you bangers and mash, and a pot of tea if you like" He thanked the man and went to sit down. Heath looked around; there was only one other guest in the pub. Quiet night, he reckoned, which was funny, considering the fact that pubs were known for having people all the time, but he thought the cold kept everyone away. The other man who was at the pub (besides the pub owner, who was working there) was elegantly dressed, in a tailored suit, near him was a brand new top-hat, which was a bit odd for a fishing village, to be seen wearing something that fancy. The elegant man didn't look very Irish he had very dark skin, brown hair, almost black, and dark eyes. You expect the Irish to be almost white, red or brown hair and blue or green eyes.

Heath blew into his hands to keep warm. "Bit nippy out, is it?" said the posh, dark skinned man.

"I can't warm up. The cold has penetrated to my bones," replied Heath Rochester. Just then the pub owner came back with the pot of tea and the food.

"That will warm you up, won't it?" said the man.

"I hope it will, I'm frozen."

"So, what brings you to Howth?" asked the dark man who was sat near Heath.

"I am an artist, I was told I would find inspiration for a painting here, or a series of paintings. English people like Irish landscapes these days, they pay really good money for them, besides, my life was a bit boring, back in York, really, things don't change in York these days. I wanted an adventure. To be honest, I used to have a big social life, I used to go to London to all the clubs, and have countless friends, we would go to the theatre and balls, and play cards, etc. Things change. Now many of them are married and have no time for social events, others have gone abroad. One of my friends went to America and now they have a civil war over in America, don't they? I decided one day that I would go as far as Ireland so now I am here." said Heath. Rochester was a single man of somewhat large fortune, and by large fortune I mean that his parents have money, but it doesn't belong to him, the money belongs to his parents, however he never lacked in anything but having said that his family always encouraged modesty. It was best to have people think you have less money than you really do.

Life in England got boring for Heath especially since he would read about people going abroad, to places like India, or Russia, etc, and in York, it's not that not much changed, with railways it was easier to travel, but when you are single and more and more of your friends have time for there families and less and less time for you, it feels as if life was not changing, besides, as an artist most of York knew about his work, but nobody in Ireland did, and Heath wanted to be known beyond York. People back home would say things like "Don't bother going to Ireland, nobody has heard of you there." Or "How are you going to sell paintings in a country where you don't know a single person?" that sort of thing but none of those words could persuade him to stay put, quite the opposite, actually, for our friend Heath, Ireland was the land of opportunity, a place where nobody was going to say hi to him because he was a Rochester, but rather he was just another artist from England, and that is exactly what he wanted.

"Oh you are an artist. Grand! I love art. I could never paint. I admire those who can. I cook and bake, but I don't paint." Said the strange, dark man.

"Well I paint and I don't cook," said Heath with a smile.

"So, can I see your paintings? Do you have them with you?" Asked the man, wanting to know more.

"I hardly ever travel with my paintings, sadly, to much of a hassle. I have photos of them though and I've an envelope with a few watercolours, would you like to see them?"

"Have you? Yea, that would be grand." Heath pulled out an envelope full of photos.

"Oh I like this one, so I do. The moon, you've made it seem almost as big as the mountains. Tell me, what medium do you use?"

"That one is a watercolour, though I prefer oils. If you make a mistake on oils, you can correct it, I always make mistakes." Heath was feeling excited, here was a man that looked very well to do, glancing at his paintings with keen interest.

"And that one?" Said the posh man, as he went through the photographs.

"Oh that's Leeds Castle. I love castles."

"As do I.," said he with a bigger smile than before. The posh man studied the photo of the painting for what seemed like quite some time.

"You know, I sold that painting, Leeds Castle, to an American, him and his family were traveling and they ran into me. His daughter, Daisy saw it. I wasn't entirely done with it, actually, the American was in a hurry, so he said he gave me what money he had, and took it unfinished."

"But it looks finished."

"Look at the foreground, it was March when I was there, the daffodils were in bloom, and I wanted them in the foreground, if you notice there is just grass there."

There was a moment of silence, as the man observed the photo more closely. Heath kept quiet, as his new friend started looking at the rest of the photos, then all of a sudden the stranger spoke. "Oh, a Wisteria, I love that flower. I used to have it growing all over my walls, but I had to cut it down. You see, the roots were growing too big, they can damage the walls, you know."

"That's a shame. They give such pretty, purple flowers, and I love the way they look on old buildings."

"And my house is very old, about as old as Leeds Castle, so it is."

There was something very mysterious about this man, he was far too formally dressed for a small, Irish, fishing village, and when he looked at the photos, he refused to come to the light, as if he preferred the darkness to the light, yet he carried himself like a count or a duke. There was also something in his smile. You know how with some people, you don't know what they are thinking when they smile? Was his smile hiding a frown or sadness, perhaps sorrow? Whatever it was, he did not seem happy.

"I love old houses. My house in England isn't that old, I wish I had an old house, like yours. Maintaining them must be a challenge, though." Said Heath Rochester. It was true. His house, though big enough, was not a castle. Close to where Heath lived, there was a castle called Castle Howard, which was one of the greatest in all of England. And north of where he lived, in Ripon, there was that place where the mad woman lived. When Heath was a child the governess would tell tales about a mad woman locked up in the attic. Heath lived in a somewhat old house in York, quite big, his house was, but it was not as interesting as Castle Howard, nor was it as astonishing as the castle in Ripon.

"You know, you must come and see my house it's nearby, it's called Clongriffin Castle."

"My word, a castle, and are you a or a lord or something?"

"No, I'm Eamon LeFroy, my family has been here since the Norman Invasion."

"Eamon LeFroy, pleased to meet you, I am Heath Rochester, from York. No title to my name, no castles, just Heath from York. And tell me, not to be rude, but on another subject, it's getting rather dark, and it's winter, as you know, do you happen to have an idea where I might find a place to stay for the night?"

"Well you can't go back to Dublin City Centre, not at this hour. There are no cabs to take you all the way to Dublin tonight. Stay at my place, you can have the grey room."

"No, I wouldn't want to be a bother, I mean I can stay in the village, and maybe see your castle tomorrow. Surely there is some place I could stay here in the village, or at a nearby one, just for the night. "

"There's no places in this village worth staying, not at this hour anyway, besides, I've a fire, and you would have a large room all to yourself, you wouldn't be in the way."

Just then the owner of the pub heard what was going on and said "Mr. LeFroy is right, it's too late at night, and there's no hotels here, not for miles. You'd best stay at his castle. I've stayed at it before, just, Oh I don't like the Grey room, not enough sunlight comes to that one room." One could tell the pub owner looked nervous when he heard about the Grey Room.

"Well if I must stay there," said Heath a bit thankful, but also a bit worried, yet thing is, he wasn't worried so much as he didn't really know Mr. LeFroy, and if you stay at a castle, they are full of antiques, and Heath was very clumsy, supposing something would break, he would be out on the street in the dead of winter. Then again, if he didn't go, he would also be out in the street anyway, for the pub was about to close for the night.

LeFroy answered to the pub owner's comment regarding the grey room, "Nonsense! Grey room has more than enough light. It has that massive window on the side and you can look out to a very small part of the garden from there."

The pub owner just nodded. He wanted to say, "Look Mr. Englishman, I've stayed there before, and it's frightening." but he did not have a chance. Our guests grabbed their things and left before he could say anything.

That said, Heath joined LeFroy and off they went to Clongriffin Castle. The ride over there was quite something, as back then, it was mostly wooded area, with not that many houses around, just farms, for the most part and forest, besides at such a late hour, everyone in the town was asleep.

The next day, Heath woke up, but he felt strange, like when you don't know if you had an experience that was a dream, or if it was real. "Am I in a castle? How did I make it here?" He had a lot of questions to ask. As Heath got up slowly, he looked out the window, there was a thick fog, it was cold out, as well, and he could sense that. Pretty soon though, he got dressed and went down for breakfast, although he really didn't want to go down for breakfast in the castle because his bed was warm and everything else was cold, but you can't be rude and stay in bed all day especially if you are the guest of someone you have just met.

"Hello." said Heath to a servant that was waiting for him downstairs as he walked down for breakfast.

"Oh, Mr. Heath, you are expecting Mr. Lefroy, are you?" said she, when she noticed that Heath was still as if in a daze.

"I was, yes"

"Oh, there's no use finding him here, he has gone down to the village early in the morning. I have had breakfast made for you, just the same, and you are to stay here for the day if you like. Mr. LeFroy has asked if you would care for a tour of the castle later on."

"If it's not a bother." Heath Rochester looked around the place. "So it wasn't all a dream then?" he thought He saw the furniture and antiques and thought it best not to touch anything.

"He insists, and besides, I suspect you like antiques, do you, Mr. Heath, or am I to call you Mr. Rochester?"

"I do like antiques, indeed, and I am sure there are several I would love to see. There are a great many stories in this castle as well. And call me Heath. My father, when he is tremendously angry with me, calls me Rochester, but I am dying to know all the stories and secrets regarding the castle." Said Heath with a smile. He was finally waking up now that they had brought his coffee and food, and he was realizing that last night was not a dream at all. "Blimey, I am in a castle, aren't I? How'd I end up 'ere." He thought.

The housekeeper got quiet for a minute, she nearly dropped a pot of coffee she had in her hand. When Heath asked about stories the castle had to say. There were several stories in this castle, not all of them lovely but perhaps she could hide those from our dear friend from York, actually, come to think of it, some of the happenings in the castle were quite scary, really, but as long as the guest didn't find out about them, all would be great.

Heath saw that the housekeeper was upset, so he said, "You know, I am sure I can wander the castle alone, a tour would be a bit of a bother, wouldn't it?"

"Not a bother at all." Said she in a quiet voice.

The housekeeper and he left for the tour after breakfast, which started, actually, at the dining room, where breakfast had been served. Heath looked at the antiques, and the art. "Ah a Francisco de Zurbaran painting." He said, as he stared at the big painting in the room.

"Not an original, though, although I am glad you recognize it. You are an educated man." The housekeeper was surprised, because most people don't know much about foreign artists, much less 17th century Spanish ones.

"Yes, a Spanish painter, I know his work well, although this is a still life, he didn't paint many of them. I am astonished, actually as this is a copy of one of his lesser known works"

"There is an artist in Dublin that does copies of works, mostly Baroque art." said she.

"Copies of original pieces of art? Is that legal? I mean, wouldn't the artist dislike the idea?"

"He doesn't do copies of art from *living* artists, not that I know of, only of artists that are now dead and whose art is now quite valuable, for example if you can't afford an original work by a seventeenth century artist he will gladly paint a copy of it."

"Well he is talented, regardless, and by the way, so art from dead artists, is it?"

"Yes, thing is, the originals, for the most part are in museums or in stately homes, and people want art that looks like what they saw in the museum. This artist has made quite a name for himself"

"My word, has he indeed? I am impressed," said Heath as he thought about the famous artist that did very good copies of art that is now found in museums.

There were other antiques in the dining room, though, like the old chandelier brought from Bohemia, and the fine china or the incredibly old pieces of furniture, but nothing as grand as the painting. The furniture looked incredible as well, but some of it was new. For example, the table must have been from the Georgian period, and the chairs were quite recent. Eamon's grandmother, when she became a widow, sold a lot of the furniture and bought new pieces, which were brought to the castle upon her death. See, not all of Eamon's family lived in the castle. His grandparents from his mother's side lived as far as Derry, but when his grandfather died, they brought his grandmother to Howth and then upon her death the furniture that she had bought was added to the castle's collection. Other pieces were old but the painting was by far the masterpiece of the dining room, even if it was a copy.

After staring at the dining room they wandered into the next room, "I see Mr. LeFroy has art from India, not everyone does."

"There was a lady that my sister used to mind, an elderly English lady who had traveled to several countries. She knew Mr. Lefroy's family well and when she died, her children, well they didn't like Indian art, it was not at all their style, you see, so they brought it over to the LeFroy family as a gift." Most of it is from India, but not all of it. Some of it is Persian art."

"Well I think it's all beautiful. I've never been to India, must be very hot there, and quite noisy, I hear, but this collection of Indian Art is quite impressive, I must say, what are your thoughts on it, Miss…?

"Victoria"

"Ah, like our current queen"

"Yes, well, one day Ireland will separate, and she won't be my queen." said Victoria, in a stern voice. "let us not discuss politics though, as, you and I would never agree on anything when it comes to politics." She continued as they went to the next room. Victoria was right, though. Heath was an Englishman who rather liked Queen Victoria and the staff member, Victoria, hated the Queen and didn't trust English people at all. Not only that, but it was seen in Ireland that when the potato famine happened, Queen Victoria did nothing to help the starving Irish and that made people very angry to say the least. What the housekeeper did not know was, Heath was a modern man, a liberal, and very much a forward thinking person and he agreed that the way The Crown handled the Irish holocaust was very badly done. However, he couldn't talk about the subject because he could tell that the housekeeper, Victoria, still had strong feelings on the subject.

"Ah, several religious paintings, I see Mr. LeFroy is a Catholic." Said Heath trying to change the subject, and noticing the other works of art.

"Yes, everyone here is."

"I am glad you are. It is important to believe in something, isn't it?" York is mostly protestant, but Scotland has Catholics. Have you been to Scotland?"

"No, I can't say I have been there. I don't think I would like to go on boats. I prefer dry land, you see, and one does need to take a boat in order to get to Scotland. Besides, I wouldn't know what to do if I went."

"Oh I'm going to have to disagree with you, there. Scotland has plenty to do, like visiting the ancient castle of Edinburgh, for example. Or you could go to Orkney. I love Orkney. Ages ago, I had a watercolour teacher, his sister lived in Orkney. Besides, it's not that long of a boat ride to Scotland, and people there are friendly, for the most part, very welcoming."

"I wouldn't know, I try not to think of wandering beyond Howth. Wouldn't want to get lost somewhere. And, truth is, I get an upset belly when I travel by boat.

My father once took us to the Isle of Man, my sisters and I, that is. I was unwell the entire trip. Something about the sea makes me unwell."

That said, they walked, through the castle, looking at all the works of art, and all the antiques, all the sculptures, etc. Victoria would mention stories of the LeFroy family, and how they had come to possess such works of art. Little did our friend Heath know though that some of the works had a dark secret to them, so when he asked about who brought what to the castle, and what there lives were like, Victoria would avoid saying things like "that's haunted" or "that's cursed". Thing is, you don't say those things to your guests, do you? There were things that had happened in the castle though, like the gas lamps turning off on their own, or objects moving about without anyone to move them, or, the scariest event was when all the paintings on the walls fell without explanation. It was one night when LeFroy had guests over. His friend Dolly was in town and they were playing cards. It was late in the evening when they heard bang, bang, bang and looked around, and there were all the paintings on the floor. It happened so fast it was hard to explain. Dolly and Lefroy walked through the entire castle that evening and saw that every single painting had fallen on the floor. Nobody knew how that happened, and nobody dared speak of it to anybody but Victoria, not even now.

The tour did end after a while, and Heath thanked Victoria for her time and wondered when Mr. LeFroy might be back, to which he was told that after six he would be, and he would meet him then at that time.

Let me tell you, dear reader, the story of a few of these works of art. There was, for example, the sculpture of Christ, brought from a trip to Spain by Mr. LeFroy;s father on a journey that he made before Eamon was born. An artist under the reign of Queen Isabel, the Catholic Queen, made the Sculpture when she wanted to convert the Muslims in the 15th century. Behind it there used to be an ancient cloak that was worn by Spanish priests hundreds of years ago, but it was no longer there, as it had burnt in a fire. The statue of Christ was never damaged, but the cloak burned till there was nothing left. The fire started when Eamon (about two decades ago, now) was going to visit his brother in Derry. Back then there was no train from Dublin to Derry and the roads were in a bad condition, so the journey was long and difficult. Heath's mother was a devout woman, went to mass every day, and she said a rosary by the statue of Christ, while her son was traveling. The problem was, she lit a candle right next to the cloak and it went up in flames, the cloak did. Mrs. LeFroy was frightened, and had the staff take out the fire. Some thought it was a bad omen, a fire burning a priest's cloak during a rosary session, People believed in bad omens in those days, but alas, there was nothing to it, the fire was put out, the cloak was burnt and was tossed away, and the statue of Christ was miraculously untouched by the flames. People did speak, however, about the statue of Christ being unharmed by the fire. Imagine this: the priest's cloak was burnt until nothing was left of it, and the statue which went up in flames as well, was left as if nothing ever happened to it. In Howth people claimed it was a miracle, and for a while everyone wanted to see the statue that was never destroyed by fire. People talked about the statue for a very long time. They were puzzled about how it looked as if it had never been on fire, yet the cloak behind it went up in flames and not a bit of it could be rescued. Some folk said it was a witch had caused the priest's cloak to burn, others that it was a demon, but in reality it was only that a candle had been kept too close to it.

Among the other works of art were three John Constable paintings, which were given to the family by a man who owed them money and had bought the paintings from Constable, back when he was an art student. Now that Constable had died, the paintings had gone up in value, although Eamon had no desire of selling them. People that came to the castle though would frequently ask how much he wanted for the paintings, but Eamon really liked the works of art and you don't sell something you like if you have no need to sell it. People wanted to buy everything, though. Just the other day a lady that was well known in Howth and knew how much the castle itself was worth wondered if LeFroy was interested in selling it. But he thanked her for her time, and he told her that he had no need to sell the castle. Sadly not everybody had been as nice as this lady, when she was told that the house was not for sale, she left but others had asked about the value of this or that artifact and when they were told that it wasn't for sale they found ways of taking certain objects, later on to have them sold in the black market.

Back to the art that was in the castle, there was also a drawing of the Virgin Mary in one of the rooms in Clongriffin Castle, done by a Spanish artist, during the time of the Inquisition. The monarchy in Spain invested a lot of money in paintings and sculptures with religious themes to them, in order to convert their subjects throughout the kingdom. This particular drawing was small, but beautiful. It was an image of the Holy Virgin, dressed in 17th century clothing, and with baby angels all around her. The drawing of the Virgin was kept in a small corner. Heath asked why, and was told that since it had been a family possession these last two centuries, at least, were it to go missing, LeFroy would never forgive himself, so he keeps it in a dark corner, in hope that very few people well see it, and thus not feel the need to steal it. The painting had gone up in value because it was now viewed as a Spanish Baroque piece worthy of being in a museum and since it was very small and amazingly well done it was considered a rare piece.

Other works of art included antique and out of print books. The library was enormous, with thousands of books on many subjects, but I don't want to bore you, dear reader, with the stories regarding every single item in the castle.

Chapter 2

Six pm came, and soon afterwards showed up Eamon LeFory. "How was your day?' he asked his guest, as Heath Rochester sat by the fire, holding a whiskey on this long winter night.

"It was good. I got a tour of the house. Victoria was kind enough to show me around. I love your castle I do not stay in castles often. "

"And you saw all the paintings, did you?" asked LeFroy as he sat in a corner of the room, away from the fire, his clothes still wet from the rain. Heath Rochester wondered why Eamon had no sense to get changed into some dry clothes before coming to say hi.

"Yes! You have a great collection. I hope to become a great painter one day. It is difficult for artists to get noticed, especially nowadays that there are so many artists and sadly, not enough buyers. You almost have to make yourself ridiculous to be noticed". What Heath Rochester said was true, the art world was changing rapidly then. People were buying art that was seen as less perfect, and more badly done or with more mistakes, and hanging this imperfect art in grand hotels and such. You see, before, art had to be perfect, structured, organized and it needed to have a theme to it, say Greek Mythology or the life of a saint. But now there were artists that did not have the skill that other artists before them had. Some of them were doing things like paint a pile of pancakes with no story behind it besides the fact that it was a painting of pancakes. Sometimes there were even a swiftly done paintings with obvious mistakes, older people hated this new art, but younger people loved it.

Heath heard once about a man, perhaps in Paris, but he could not recall where. This artist had taken a canvas and covered it in black paint with no detail to it at all, just the black paint, then put a horrible title to it. But, in reality Heath doubted that such a thing had ever happened, because there is little merit in that. However, he did know of a man in London that had made a painting of a donkey and called it "self-portrait". Well when London Society saw it, folks nearly fainted, some even threw their hats at it in protest. Heath was not that ridiculous, he took his art very seriously indeed, but he did not know how to sell it to people that were not his friends. See, there are two types of artists: those that no matter how good or bad they are, they are they have all the right contacts that they sell everything they do, but then there are 90% of all artists that can be extraordinary, but not have the contacts to become known. And this was Heath.

When it came to selling art, Heath knew some people, back in York, but what happens is the following: If you go to York and want a painting, there are only a handful of artists there, and they all know each other, so you either buy art from one artist or another, but your options are limited. However, if you go abroad, chances are you will encounter more artists, so although Heath Rochester was known in York, as one of the most celebrated artists there, he was not known beyond York, and the big art centres of the world were not—sadly-- in York.

"Well your work speaks wonders to me. You must let me show it to some of my friends in Dublin, that is, if you don't mind?" said LeFroy to Rochester. And LeFroy was right, Heath's art was incredible, the thing was, only a handful of people knew about it.

Heath couldn't refuse that offer, since, wanting to be noticed is his goal, and the thought of having Dublin's elite look at his paintings was a serious matter to him. Imagine, having paintings in castles, or large country houses that would be a dream come true. But that's not all that was on his mind, as the two of them sat by the fire. Our friend, Heath also thought of the castle he was currently in. He had never been a guest in a castle in Ireland before. Gather, he had been a guest in a castle, but not in Ireland, and the feel to it was slightly different than to castles in England. Rochester could not explain it, but everything felt different, and besides, the furniture and antiques and works of art fascinated him, and how old everything was. Heath felt hypnotized by it, in a way. I don't know if any of you, dear readers, have had that one fairy tale moment when you walk into a room or a very elegant hotel and it just oozes elegance, far greater than what you are used to? That was what Heath was feeling. Heath Rochester came from an upper income family, but although they had valuables in his home, they were considered new rich and grand castles were still foreign enough to him.

Heath and Eamon talked for hours, about what it was like to own a castle, and about what life was like in old York, and all sorts of things they talked about, until it was well past bedtime. Victoria had left a couple hours earlier as she had work in the early morning and was no longer needed that night. Finally, when Heath could not possibly stay awake, he asked to be shown to his room.

The room was a magnificent one. Why they called it the grey room was beyond him because everything was in bright colours. In reality it was more like something you might expect in Spain or Peru than in Ireland. The walls were a bright lemon yellow, there was an old birdcage of rococo design made about a century or so ago in the corner, then there was the wardrobe, a French Baroque one, and a bed, which was lavish and elegant. Above the bed was a painting of Christ, which-- as pretty as it was-- it seemed to not fit well. As if the person who put it there did not think of the size of the wall or the decorations which would complement the painting. But no matter, it was a very beautiful painting. See, the painting was very small and the wall was quite big, so the painting looked a lot smaller than it actually was. Had the same painting been put elsewhere, or with other paintings, it would not have looked out of place. But lesson for us all, don't put a miniature painting all alone in a massive wall and not centred properly because one's mind will wonder what's going on.

That night, as he lay in bed, Heath Rochester heard the most awful noise, a Banshee, he thought. He had heard that in Ireland there existed such a creature, and although he didn't believe in them, he clearly heard the cry of one. Heath couldn't sleep that night, thinking what a horrible noise that was. It was a terribly cold night as well. Heath wondered if the unbearable cold and the loud scream were related to each other in some way. The Banshee is a strange creature, and it is said to do unheard of things. Imagine yourself in bed in a strange castle in a country you have never been to, trying to get a good night's sleep when out of nowhere you hear a scream as if someone were in severe pain, that is what our friend Rochester woke up to that night. He did go back to sleep however he wondered what the noise was.

The next morning came, though, and Heath was at breakfast when Eamon and he were talking. "Eamon, my friend, did you hear that noise last night? That horrid noise, almost as if someone had been murdered right in front of me."

"Oh it was just the cats, screeching," said Eamon. "You know how they are"

Heath knew very well what cats are like, and he also knew when he was being lied to, and that was one of those moments. Cats, indeed, don't make that deafening noise. See, for those of you not aware, when felines fight they do make an awful sound, or when they cry, but this was high pitched and nothing like a "meow, I am frozen please let me in" sort of cry. It was more like person, perhaps a woman going "Oh Dear God, I am in horrible pain" sort of noise, and nothing at all like a cat would make. At least not the cats in England. Alas, if LeFroy wouldn't talk about that horrid noise, perhaps Victoria would.

Rochester hurried with his breakfast and asked if he could see Victoria because he wanted to borrow a book. Eamon LeFroy rang for her, and she came at once. Eamon apologized that he could not help Heath look for a book, but he said he had to go to Dublin again, on a matter of urgent business, so he grabbed his things and left.

Eamon was a strange man indeed. He was very friendly, but he always seemed to be going somewhere and always in a hurry, yet when you asked him where he was headed, he never said where. LeFroy would only answer "yes" or "no".

Victoria was now alone with Heath, as soon as Eamon left, and they were finally able to talk.

"A book?" asked she "any subject in particular? We have thousands of books" They did have thousands of books. Actually, the family of LeFroy used to love to read, so they had collected books for centuries, and they rarely threw any away. The LeFroy's also had a habit of collecting books that people in Dublin would discard, so when you have centuries collecting books, in time you have a very huge library. Eamon himself loved to read, as did his father before him and between the two of them, their already large collection grew enormously. A little bit about the books, though. The collection began several centuries ago and back then getting certain books to Ireland was difficult in part because Ireland was considered so far away but also because back then not everybody in Ireland could read so there was no point in importing books from abroad, unlike now, where everybody in Ireland reads. The thing is, the LeFroy family for hundreds of years went through great lengths to get books. That is in part why books were rarely tossed out in the castle, but that was a good thing because now, centuries later, there was a collection of thousands of pieces of literature on countless subjects.

"Anything on ghosts, goblins, spirits, demons? That sort of thing?" asked Heath, inquiring about the books.

"You heard her scream too, then?" Victoria asked Heath "I told you, even the furniture had stories, when I gave you the tour of the castle, yesterday. You see, in the early years of the last century, Mr. Lefroy's ancestors, one of them, he shot himself here in this house, at a Christmas party. They say his ghost wanders the place, and the cries you heard are his cries from hell."

"But that sounded like a woman, did it not?" Heath didn't believe for an instant that somebody's ghost could be heard from beyond the grave. It was absurd; once you are dead, you most certainly do not make noise, much less shout at people as they slept, it is not proper to shout at people while they were at rest. What Victoria had read though, was that the Devil, or a demon can take any shape. They say that one day it can be a school boy, the next, an old person, and so on. Plus, it can trick you. Demons love tricks. One trick it does is to make you think you hear a child or a woman but you turn around and see a man. Or, for instance, you think someone is calling you, then you turn around and nobody is to be found. At any rate, the sound was that of a woman screaming and Heath wanted to find out why.

"It could be his wife, or perhaps one of his daughters. Tragedy has been in this house for a long while, but it's about time you know the story, let us sit down". As they sat, she began talking. "You see, many centuries ago, the family of LeFroy came over from France when the

Normans came and they were penniless then. You always hear about the grand Norman invaders, but along with them there were people whose lives had not amounted to much, and they saw opportunity abroad. Some of the members of the LeFroy family were highwaymen, others were prostitutes, and so on, but one day, someone became very wealthy, very fast. They say there's a golden treasure hidden beneath this castle. No one knows for sure, but what we do know is that the family is full of lunatics, and such. Not Eamon, no, he is perfectly normal. But some other relatives, some say the spirits from Hell wander these walls, and protect the gold, others, that it's a banshee, that guards the gold, while others say the story of the gold was made up. I don't believe it, however, some people have found priceless treasures on the hill in Howth. Another thing, whenever anyone is going to ask about the treasure, she appears, the woman with the horrible screams."

"Well I don't want it; I have enough money, thanks, and have never had need for more. I have learned that money doesn't provide happiness. A whole bunch of gold, I wouldn't know what to do with it, to be honest. I want to be happier, not wealthier."

"I doubt it's YOU, she is worried about, but you see, I can tell you are a very kind, innocent man and it's no accident that Mr. LeFroy found you in Howth, let's just say he needs an innocent, good hearted friend."

"Found me? "

Heath thought about everything, why was he at the castle? I mean besides the fact that he needed shelter that one night. But he felt in a way, that he was meant to be there. He was also enchanted by the whole experience. Thing is, here he was, an English man, in faraway Howth, in Ireland, in a castle called Clongriffin Castle, also known as LeFroy's Castle, and it all seemed strange, yet familiar to him at the same time. Everything did. Like when you happen to go to a place you have obviously never been to, yet you already know your way around? Or when you meet someone for the first time, but you feel like you had been friends forever? That, dear readers, is what Heath Rochester felt when in he was in the castle. Heath also thought about LeFroy, because you see, Eamon kept as many secrets as he did antiques, and he had a large amount of both.

"I see you are in deep thought, Mr. Rochester, Sr. Are you frightened by ghosts?"

"No. I don't think I believe in them, at least I didn't until now. I mean, I do remember when I was a child my mother took me to a house that she claimed was haunted. She said that in the castle there was a man that had married a lunatic, so he locked her up in the attic, but I never heard nor saw anything, so I thought my mother was trying to scare me, really. I heard that other people in this place called Ripon would mention the mad woman in the attic, but I just thought it was all made up. Really, I have never actually seen a ghost."

"Clongriffin Castle holds many secrets. Nobody is the same once they discover them, and if you think a story about a mad woman in England is scary hold on to your hat, this castle is far spookier than that."

Heath felt like he was already changed. One day he was preparing a trip to Ireland, the next he was in a mysterious castle that was seemingly haunted. Heath felt the urge to investigate the horrible cries at night, but he was also here to paint, though. And that afternoon, paint is exactly what he did, investigating mysteries would happen soon enough.

Regarding painting, Heath Rochester did not have a lot of materials with him but he had enough. And he was given access to a room where he could look out at the trees and paint them without getting wet. It was very cold and rainy that day. A wind had blown in from Russia over Scandinavia and had caused the weather in Ireland to turn painfully cold and wet. Heath did not know what to paint at first. He looked out the window and saw the grey clouds and the rain, so he painted that, but he had trouble concentrating, as his mind would wander constantly.

Night came, though and Heath was back in his room, reading a book about cursed objects, wondering if the banshee, or whatever that thing was, would come again, when he heard a nock at his door. Which startled him. "Who is it?" he asked.

"Hi, Heath, it's me" said Eamon LeFroy. "Listen, I wanted to ask you if you wouldn't be bothered by another guest in this house? You see, my cousin is coming from Galway tomorrow morning, Jane is her name, and, I think you and her would get along quite well. She is twenty, and has no friends in these regions. I was wondering if you could keep her company?"

"I haven't got many friends here either, so yes, not a bother at all."

"Grand, then, she arrives after breakfast, so." Breakfast, Heath had come to learn, was served early in LeFroy castle. Back in England, Heath Rochester was known to wake up later than expected because he had no children and he had no reason to wake up early but he had noticed that Eamon LeFroy woke up quite early, so Rochester would make an effort to be at breakfast especially early the next day.

Eamon left Heath for the night, and then the darkness came. There was the horrible cry of the Banshee or spirit, or whatever it was, but only once, although it must have played with Heath's mind, for he had the most horrible dream after the shout was heard. In his dream, he was in a park, back in England, and he sat, at a picnic with other people around him, when all of a sudden, he was staring at death itself. It was very strange indeed, because it started peaceful, a picnic, jolly good fun. He was talking to a lady and her child, when death appeared and took him away. Heath got up in an instant, he was nervous. It's like the spirit of death had followed him to England, but then realized it was time for breakfast anyway, and he needed to get dressed and go downstairs.

Heath Rochester was in deep thought as he got dressed, he thought about the dream of his death in a park back in England. He wondered who the woman was and who the child was. He was also taken by the fact that in the dream he looked older, not elderly but more mature looking, as if the dream were a vision of the future and that is indeed how he was to die. But then he tried talking sense to himself, as it were and said "It can't mean anything, the dream has to be meaningless."

Heath put his clothes on and went down for breakfast, where he saw Eamon and Victoria, who had just brought the tea. "Ah, your cousin arrives soon, doesn't she?" Heath asked his new friend LeFroy.

"Yes, one of my staff members has already gone for her at the train station. "Eamon wasn't in the best of moods, Heath thought, or perhaps he too had bad dreams. One could see in his eyes that something was upsetting him. Rochester decided not to chat for too long for fear of putting Eamon in a grumpy mood, so he ate his breakfast rather quickly. As he was about to finish with his meal, though, the door flung open and a youthful figure walked in, a gorgeous, young woman, dressed in red satin; red was *the* fashionable colour back then. The dress is worth talking about, though, it was, as mentioned, red satin but it went from a dark red at the top to a lighter red at the bottom and it was wide and gorgeous. Jane had blond hair and lovely eyes although from where Rochester was sat he could not tell if they were green or blue, but she had it in a fashion which looked like something that the Normans would have used. Jane also had a ruby necklace with black stones. Was it black jade, Heath wondered.

"Oh cousin" Jane said in a smile. "I must tell you all about my trip. Would you believe how fast trains go these days? I hate to think what could be invented that could go faster." She was going to say more, when she saw Heath, His brown eyes glancing at her captured Jane's attention. Her eyes sparkled and looked like some jewel or elegant crystal when she glanced at him.

"Hello, I'm Jane, you must be Heath. My cousin told me you are staying in the grey room. I find that room boring, not much to look at besides an old birdcage. Is that birdcage in the corner still there? Our auntie brought it from Italy once, or was it Spain? I'm in the next room, by the bye, the one that's near the library. I can sneak in and grab a book at night, something scandalous, I hope, like Tom Jones. Have you read Tom Jones?"

"Yes, I have read Tom Jones, indeed. And Are you not afraid of wandering these dark walls at night?"

"Not in my room, no, I stayed in your room once and had nightmares every single night, I can't tolerate nightmares, they frighten me. I sleep soundly in the other room, though."

"So, you had nightmares? I have them as well. Horrible, that room is. Isn't it?"

"I heard a woman was murdered in that room, like a century or so ago, and ever since haunts whoever stays in there." Said Jane

"Don't be silly" said Eamon who was hearing the conversation. "There's no such thing as ghosts." Eamon had been quiet this whole time, until now. He hated the talk of ghosts. LeFroy would get in the worst of moods when he would hear about ghosts, demons or anything of that sort.

"Oh I think there are ghosts. There's no point in owning a castle, if there's no ghosts or demons in it." Said Jane, to her cousin. "Gather, I could never afford a castle, I'm not wealthy, like you are, and castles aren't free these days, are they?" continued she. Heath was relieved to see Jane. Her energy was like a breath of fresh air in such a damp, dark place. Jane was like a bubble of glee.

Whatever the truth was regarding the ghost, now Heath was curious to say the least in order to find out what was going on in this castle but at least he had an ally this time. Both Jane and him could find time to search the castle for answers. Unfortunately though, that day there would be no time for searching the castle. Eamon LeFroy thought it best to have a picnic in the garden. Victoria called the rest of the staff of the castle, (which I had not mentioned much until now) to get to help set things up for the picnic. Eamon wanted his two guests to have tea near the forest area.

As the household staff was setting things up for the picnic, Heath realized he had not seen the gardens yet so he set out to walk in the garden. "My word, the garden is bigger than the castle." This part was true, the castle was big, but the gardens were huge.

"Oh and you haven't seen all of it, there's the woods beyond the garden, that are great for exercise and fresh air. You need to take a walk there one day, it's well worth it." Said LeFroy

"I am in need of exercise, aren't I?" replied Heath, as he grabbed another piece of the cake. "I also think I would like to paint this landscape. " but how big are the grounds, if you don't mind my asking?"

"Well, enormous but, before I forget, Heath, I was thinking, there's these men in town I happen to know, some friends of mine, and thing is, how would you like to show your paintings to them? I think someone has a gallery near Marion Square. I mean, you did come to Ireland to paint the Irish landscape, but what if I put you in contact with a few people..." Eamon wasn't done speaking, when Heath got visibly exited.

"WOW, a gallery in Marion Square? That's fantastic, yes; I would indeed love to go. Perhaps your cousin, Jane, would love to join us."

"Oh that sounds like fun. There's an antique shop nearby, at least there was, last time I was in Dublin. There's a portrait I like to look at there. I hope it hasn't sold. It's the one they used to put next to the window, the big one." Commented Jane.

"Grand! The three of us can go, day after tomorrow" said Eamon

"Why not tomorrow?" Asked Jane

"Well tomorrow I am in Howth all day. I've things to do, but you know, Heath, you were only in Howth at night, weren't you? You need to see it in the day, there's the train station that's about 20 years old or so, and the harbor. It was built before I was born, but not long before, and the abbey, Howth has an abbey as well. You need to go up and see it."

"Sounds like fun. I am sure Jane could show me around"

"I love Howth, such a small village, yet so near Dublin. The only thing I don't care for much is the walk form there to Sutton." Jane said.

"Listen, you will be grand, no one ever died, walking from Howth to Sutton." said Eamon

"I am sure we will be fine," said Heath, with a big smile.

"Heath, you mentioned how big the gardens were, well you won't believe it, when the castle was built, the nearby villages were incredibly small, only a house here and there, and some of them didn't exist until much later, so my ancestors bought an impossible amount of land, that's why there's far more garden than castle, really. Victoria has advised me to sell some of it to developers, but I couldn't think of anything worse than having suburbs in Clongriffin, besides, it's too far from everything, It won't happen in my lifetime." said Eamon

"I don't know." Mentioned Jane" The rest of Dublin is too far, but one day, it will grow out this way"

"As far as Clongriffin, nonsense! Next you will tell me they will put suburbs in Malahide. Don't be ridiculous, Jane." said her cousin. The idea of Dublin expanding as far as Clongriffin seemed ridiculous to LeFroy.

That conversation over and done with and the picnic came to an end, as it began to get dark and tremendously cold and Heath began to worry. He dreaded the nightmares.

When night came, Heath took his things off and went to bed and his fear came true. As he was in bed, he heard noises; at first he thought it was just the wind and rain, but then he wasn't sure. Our English friend used to not believe in goblins and fairies and such things, but those cries at night, it was like the cry of death. Perhaps spirits did exist and thing is, these cries did mean something, for some reason they seemed to only happen in this very room, but why Eamon denied them, was beyond him.

Heath heard the horrible cries, and he got out of bed, and looked around. He knew he couldn't see the spirit but there was something there, he could feel it. Heath's spine was tingling as if someone was looking at him breathing on him almost, only there was nobody to be found. There were just old books and paintings in the room, and that old birdcage, nothing alarming. He knew, however, that he had seen a photograph of the same room earlier, perhaps in the morning he could look for it, maybe that could help. Sometimes photos can reveal secrets, or so Heath thought.

The next morning he rushed out of bed, and before he put his clothes on, he looked for the photograph. It was on the desk near his bed. Heath observed the photo. Where the painting of Christ is now, on the wall near the bed, there used to be what looks like a wood boat, why was it removed? And why was there an image of Christ now, where the boat was? That was the only difference between the old photograph and the way the room was currently. Heath Rochester did not know if anything he saw in the photo meant anything at all or not but he would soon find out.

After he looked at the photo, and got dressed, he went down for breakfast. Eamon wasn't down yet; apparently he hadn't slept well that night. Jane was down, however and she was looking very perky and Heath wanted to speak to her anyway. "Do you know the room I am in? "He asked 'I found a photograph of it and was there a statue of a boat or something before, a relief or wood carving, perhaps? You know, where the painting of Christ is?"

"The castle has a way of giving up its secrets. Eamon was worried you would find that photo, but, it was a wood carving of a ship that was destroyed, the real ship sunk, that is. Some of our family members drowned in it, or so I have heard. Some of our ancestors wanted to go abroad once, and they went on a ship that was supposed to go to America, anyway, the wind picked up and the ship sunk, but another boat was going by and found some people and rescued them. One of the ancestors had the wood carving of the very same boat with them, but when they came to Ireland and placed it on the wall, strange things started to happen. Gather, strange events always happened in this castle. I don't know if the boat had anything to do with it, but people said so."

"I knew this house had secrets, Victoria warned me about it."

"But how did you find it, the photo?"

"It was on the desk, couldn't have been easier to find, really."

"Oh, because last time I was here, that photo had been hidden away."

"Well it's not hidden now, is it?"

"Well I don't go into your room, no matter what." Those words being said, Eamon walked into the breakfast room where everyone was waiting. Heath was sad because he wanted to ask why the room was called the grey room, but with Eamon around, nobody would be able to chat.

"Sorry I slept in, I had a headache all last night." Eamon Lefroy did know about the spirit in the Grey room in Clongriffin Castle, he just didn't want to admit it, since he was ashamed that one of his ancestors haunted the castle. Eamon was a proud man, and wanted everything to be perfect in his life all the time and a ghost, or spirit, or banshee, or whatever it was, did indeed have a dark secret from the past and he never wanted anyone to know that some of his ancestors had been horrible. Yet Heath, the English guest, was an intelligent man and the truth would be found out. Our friend from York meant well and did not want anybody to feel shame by having secrets found out but when you have nightmares about your own death and when you hear screams at night in the very room you have dreadful dreams in. Perhaps it is wise to investigate the cause, besides the family of Rochester had deep, dark secrets too but they were buried in old England.

Heath Rochester was given a book by Victoria that afternoon. It was about spirits. As he read it he realized that when you investigate a spirit you have to be careful because, if you wake the evil spirits, every bad thing imaginable could happen. Heath thought, as he read. There was a section on good spirits and Rochester was convinced that this was a good spirit, maybe even a playful one. Nobody that was alive today had dared investigate the specter but Heath thought the following:

#1 The spirit seems to want to be found out. For example, if nobody left the picture of the room Rochester was in, it must have been him or her, or whatever it was.

#2 The religious images throughout the castle made Heath think that perhaps somebody in the past did try to investigate the ghost and they must have had a horrible time at that. So by placing images of Christ all over the place they hoped that the specter might calm down or go away... at least that was the conclusion Heath came up with.

#3 One of the chapters in the book talked about cursed vs blessed objects. Since the family of LeFroy collected antiques from all over the world, there was a possibility that one of them could have been cursed, thus introducing a spirit into the castle but by bringing in holy icons, some even brought from as far as Palestine, then there was hope that the spirit should go away. I need to explain this last point further. You see if you have a cursed object that has brought with it a malign being, a way to have the ghost go away is by bringing in a blessed object, say a rosary or a bible or an image of Christ or of some saint perhaps. It was evident to Heath R. that the reason why there were so many religious images throughout the castle was that someone had in the past tried to get rid of the evil being which had been brought into the place.

As Heath began to think, he began to write his conclusions down on paper, he thought that maybe he could find out which of all the objects in the castle was the cursed one, if any.

Another part of the book that he was reading talked about haunted houses, like in Salem in America, where there was a haunted house where the witches had once lived, or the Cathedral in Durango, Mexico, where visitors to the Cathedral frequently saw a ghost of a nun. Now Heath had two hypotheses, either a) one object was cursed, and must be removed, possibly burnt, or b) the castle itself was cursed.

Jane and Heath Rochester talked about what could possibly be the case in this haunting, as both scenarios seemed just as likely.

Chapter 3

Jane, Eamon and Heath Rochester went to Howth on that day after they had breakfast. Heath and Jane went to the village for a walk, while Eamon went to see a friend, who lived just up the hill. The ride over to Howth village was a pleasant one. Jane, by the way, was curious to know more about her new friend, Heath Rochester and so she started asking him all sorts of questions.

"So, Heath, how did you get a name like yours, in all fairness, it's not a common name"

"My parents knew a man in York, where I was born, whose family had come from as far as the Ottoman Empire and they say he was fond of me when I was a baby. When my parents were away for whatever reason he would look after my siblings and me. A great man, he was. It was he that came up with the name

Heath. It was a name he heard, or read about somewhere. I believe it was a story he came across, about a man called Heathcliff, so he shortened it. This man used to travel a lot and would hear the most interesting names that aren't terribly common. He also loved reading, so he did, and several books that he came across had characters with rather exotic names. I also learned a lot, thanks to him. His name was Aaron. And how I remember hearing about far away lands." Heath was in deep thought as he walked with Jane. He remembered old man Aaron and all the stories he would tell.

"The Ottoman Empire? WOW, I have always wanted to travel to those far away lands but now I want to know, how did that man, your parent's friend, Aaron, how did he come all the way to York and why?" asked Jane, wanting to know the whole story.

"I have absolutely no idea. His daughter worked as a governess, I remember that. Gorgeous, his daughter was. He gave her an English name because he didn't want people talking about why she had a different name."

"Oh dear, what ever happened to her?"

"Emily, was her name. There was a family in Halifax that needed a governess to work for them. You know, I haven't heard from her since she left for Halifax. I presume she finds herself well, though."

"You must visit her. Wouldn't that be fun?" Said Jane with a smile. She had heard of Halifax, but she forgot where it was located, as she had never actually been there. Jane loved hearing stories of adventure, and she wished she could travel the world over.

Heath thought for a while. He wasn't sure what he would do once he got to Halifax were he to go looking for Emily. Would he knock at people's doors to see who had a governess named Emily? Nobody would do that, although the population of the place is smaller than most places in the world. No matter, though, why would he look for someone else, when he had gorgeous Jane to look at and today especially. She was wearing a violet dress and a black coat to keep her warm during this horrid, rainy season. Her bonnet was black as well, with violet ribbons. No woman in all of Ireland could look more beautiful than she on that day. Heath thought that doing a painting of her would be a lovely idea. When he was younger Heath had studied the works of

Sr. Joshua Reynolds and Thomas Gainsborough. He remembered what his professor would say about how Gainsborough was better at landscapes, but everyone would pay him to do their portraits, and Heath Rochester was better at landscapes than at portraits. However, Jane looked gorgeous that day and he wanted to remember that walk with her forever. Heath thought of Jane as they walked, but he also remembered Emily.

Funny, though, you know how life takes so many turns. I guess you could describe them as winding roads, really. For example, Heath's childhood friend, Emily. There was a time before she left to Halifax to be a governess, that Heath could have courted her and as pretty as she was, Heath did imagine himself with her indeed. But she was more interested in being a governess, so they were never engaged, they weren't even lovers or anything. But all these years later, Heath was still single, but now staring at very beautiful Jane. Life would have possibly been lovely with Emily, had Heath been serious with her, but now he felt that life with Jane could be quite nice as well. Gather, as they say, it was early days, but just the same Jane was beautiful, and her blond locks of hair made her look like an angel.

The pair walked from Howth Harbour up the hill to Howth Abbey as they talked about this and that. Both of them loved the view from the Abbey. As they walked the grounds, it started to rain. "You know, this reminds me of Whitby. Have you been there? It's a gorgeous place, there's an abbey and the wind blows really hard all the time there and, thing is, if you stand in the middle of the Abbey, the wind tends to blow on all sides, and it sounds like ghosts howling. Also, there is a graveyard nearby, just like this one, so you get a really scary feeling. Whitby's abbey is quite similar to this one in a strange way. It's much bigger but the architecture is similar. You need to go one day, I would love to show you it." Said Heath with a smile.

"Whitby? I've never even been to England, but is Whitby big? I have seen photos of some abbeys in England and they are enormous, aren't they? Someone back home in Galway, where I am from, went once to Fountains Abbey on a trip he made to England and the photo he took made it look enormous, it did. " Jane was going to speak more, but Heath interrupted

"Sorry, I have been rude, you never told me how you got the name Jane"

"Jane? Well, I was born twenty years ago and there were Jane's everywhere then, really. There are fewer Jane's now, aren't there? I wonder where all the girls called Jane are now, are they all hiding somewhere? "

"Well in all fairness, how many Heath's do you know?" Both of them looked into each other's eyes and laughed. Jane blushed, as she stared at Heath's penetrating, brown eyes and Heath turned red as he looked into her blue eyes. "Oh look, you can see the boats form here," she said, to change the subject, hoping Rochester wouldn't notice her blush.

"Yes, I can see one come in now. I wonder if it came from a warmer climate. I often wonder about boats when I see them. I would love to go to a warmer country, maybe the West Indies, or somewhere, maybe even as far as Timbuktu." Said Heath. 'There is a place back in England called Scarborough. There is a small shop there, and the owner is a mulata from Santo Domingo and she is always mentioning the climate back home. It's what she misses most. I've an atlas in my house in York and I looked up Santo Domingo, it is remarkably far, actually, but I hear it is really pretty." Continued Heath.

"Oh, I always dream about traveling abroad. Egypt, West Indies, as you say, India, China, most countries, actually. Well your friend who named you, the man from the Ottoman Empire, it's quite warm there, isn't it?" Jane commented.

"I believe it is, well the part he was from anyway. See the empire is huge, so some parts are hot all the time, but other parts have real winter and it gets to be really, really cold. I believe he is from Palestine originally, but he told us once that they had so much heat in his hometown that they longed for rain, especially in the hot, summer months. The winter, I hear is quite different though, in Palestine, they get snow at times, although he said that they had better weather than the Arabs, and that in lands further East of him, see there are several rivers in the Empire--the Nile in Egypt, the Jordan river, which is where he was from, then the Tigris and last the Euphrates. Old Aaron would say that if you go to Egypt it can be quite hot. If you go to the area between the Tigris and Euphrates, in what used to be Mesopotamia, that is where Adam and Eve were from, well that gets terribly hot as well, but he grew up near the Jordan river and he remembered cold nights and especially cold winters."

"Is that so? I never knew that. By the bye, should we go look for my cousin now? The cold is a bit much for me, really. He said he was with a friend, Eamon did, I know this man, right, he lives a block from here, they always have tea there." Said Jane, and off they went.

For those of you not familiar with Howth, it is a very small fishing village where most people live on a hill overlooking the sea. But don't think tropical sea with palm trees. This is the Irish Sea where it rains 867 days a year and when it does not rain, there is a drizzle, so one must always be prepared for more rain and more rain. The best clothes to wear when planning a trip to Howth, is anything that will not soak through and preferably something to keep warm in as well. The people of Howth are tremendously friendly but they have a half hour of sunshine a year, so do not think you need short sleeves when you go.

The population is small in this village and they all know each other. They all go to the same pub that is not that far from the Abbey and it has been there for quite some time. Modernity is reaching Howth, for Dublin City Centre is not that far from it if one takes the train, although when the first train arrived, people thought it was too big and too loud and that it would be a failure. However, just a few years later everybody loved it.

Howth has an Abbey as well, which is in ruins. I think the Abbey goes back to the Middle Ages. There is a harbour as well and there are a few houses on the hill, not many, though. I rather doubt one would want more houses. The more people there are, the more crowded things get. The rest of the hill is green due to the rain. It is funny, though, Heath R. is from York, so he is used to the rain and the astonishingly green landscape. However, if you think England is green and rainy, Ireland is in a league all on its own. It would be hard to imagine any place on earth as green or as rainy as Ireland. More about Howth, though: one can see deer on the green area quite frequently. There is a castle on the top of the hill as well, but hardly anyone visits the top of the hill, as it is a long way up. Once at the top, on a clear day, you can see several counties in Ireland. Since very few people go that far up the hill, the people of Howth village had quite a lot of stories about the place. One of the greatest things about the green area on the hill in Howth, though, is that many of the locals enjoy having picnics there and all the children love playing there and running about on Sundays after church.

And there we find our friends, up on the hill, just leaving the Abbey and walking towards a house that had been built for the family of O'Dell, Eamon's friend. The O'Dell family had originally come from Limerick but decided to settle in Howth not that many decades ago. Remember, the hideous potato famine, also known as the Irish Holocaust, the one that Queen Victoria shamefully did nothing about? Those were tragic times when many fled Ireland and wasn't all that long ago.

Many Limerick families were very much affected by the tragic famine and were forced to leave in hoards. The O'Dell family wanted to go to England, because Martin O'Dell (at whose house everyone was now currently in) had a cousin in England and when his cousin found out that Old Martin O'Dell and his wife were suffering. He wrote to Old Martin and told him to go to England, where he and his wife would be looked after.

Life takes you places you don't expect and when the family of O'Dell was in Dublin, finding a way to get to England, one thing led to another and they ended up in

Howth, which they liked a lot, actually. Here, my readers, is where we find the current Mr. O'Dell (his wife now deceased). You see him there, with his friend Eamon LeFroy, discussing what's to be done with the garden. The rain was too strong for anyone that was indoors to dream of going out, but one can see the garden from the window, so no need to be outdoors and plan what's to be done regarding the gardening when you can be inside and decide. So there were Lefroy and O'Dell looking out at the weather, when there was a knock on the door, and in came our wet friends, Jane and Heath.

"Ah, Jane, I'm glad it's you, did you show Heath the village?"

"Yes, we got to see the Abbey, the harbour and the new train station, but it's getting dark and there's no time for the castle on top of the hill, or the tower and with this rain. "

"The Abbey was good enough for me." Said Heath with a smile, as he looked at Jane and her gorgeous eyes.

"Please, you are both cold, let me make you a cup of tea" said kind Mr. O'Dell "You must be sat by the fire to warm up." Continued he. Our friends, Heath and Jane were tremendously cold, actually, so the fire was very welcome.

The cup of tea was as lovely as was the present company. Heath was sipping his warm cup, when Mr. O Dell said "You know, Eamon has been telling me all about your paintings, you are an artist. He wants your paintings shown in Marion Square. You notice he seems to disappear quite frequently, doesn't he? That's because when he met you at the pub he got exited and wanted to show the whole world your paintings. Eamon could never draw or paint. He is good at running a castle, though, but in any case, he saw your paintings and he knows you will be famous, but you could use some help. No artist can become famous on his own."

I pause here to say, Eamon LeFroy always wanted to be an artist but he got rejected from all the great academies in Europe. However, he loved art and made it one of his goals in life to have other artists become famous. And that is why he was so taken by Heath's art-- he saw an opportunity to take a little- known artist from abroad and make his art known throughout Ireland, possibly throughout Europe as well.

"Eamon has been very kind, and truth be told, I was lucky, because I was looking for an adventure and he just happened to be in the right place at the right moment; it was cold, raining, I was frozen and walked into this one pub that had the lights on. And I think we got on well and I was more than happy to stay at his castle, gather, at first. In the beginning I was nervous. Imagine a man that you have never met in your life tells you to go to his castle. Have you heard of that man, Blackbeard, didn't he chop women up to bits, or was that Bluebeard? Either way, I did have that in the back of my mind, but LeFroy seemed so tremendously friendly and to be honest, I had no option, as there are no hotels in Howth currently and with such cold weather, I don't know what I would have done. Not only that, but I have met Jane now. She showed me around Howth, she has been so kind. I daresay I could not have had a nicer companion than her, really." Rochester looked at Jane and smiled. She sat in a corner, by the fire, looking as if she had never had a bad thought in her life.

"Oh, by the way, I stayed in Clongriffin Castle once, when I was new here, he found me much like he found you, Eamon did, my friend. But tell me he didn't put you in the damn grey room, did he?" said O'Dell.

"I am afraid so."

Mr. O Dell took a sip of tea and stared sternly at Eamon's eyes. "Heavenly Jaysus, Eamon, are you determined to put all of Europe in that room?" Eamon got upset at this, but he found nothing to say, besides, castle owners never show when they are upset or angry, it's not proper.

"I have stayed in that room a time or two, and I don't like it either," said Jane. "Everyone has nightmares, I think it's a spirit from the past that wanders there," continued she. Everybody the world over knows that all castles have spirits and goblins.

"Jane, I am miles ahead of you there. I did my own investigating and realized, there are several types of spirits, some are good, some bad, but they are real. Eamon has had a dark family history, suicides, shipwrecks, lunatics, highwaymen, prostitutes, murderers, heaven knows what else. The spectre of LeFroy's Castle is clearly one of his ancestors that's in torment in the afterlife and I often wonder if it could be someone that died there. You have had dreams there, no doubt, we all have" said O'Dell, looking at Heath.

"I saw my own death, in a park, many years from now. I was in England, but not in York, where I am from. I was in London. London was different though, I can't describe it, and it was much bigger. I keep having different variations of the same dream, and other nonsensical dreams but in this one, queen Victoria is celebrating something big, I'm old, but not very old, perhaps in my fifties or so. Anyway I go to a park, and then death stares me in the face and that's when I wake up. In one version of my dream, there was a fire, but in another one it was much more peaceful, really. I have seen other things as well. I wonder if the ghost isn't trying to tell me something. Thing is, it's more complicated than that, I'm afraid. In this one dream I was lying in a coffin in my own funeral in a medieval church that looked sort of like St. Margaret's Church in London, you know the one by St. James's Palace? But it was not like I was in my coffin all nervous like, no, it was actually quite peaceful, as if I was sleeping but I could see everybody mourn me. I also saw myself floating about the place but I was not remotely sad. Anyway, it's like I'm in my own funeral, and there's all these people there, I recognized some of them as well. Some people in my funeral are people I know quite well, but others, I have no clue who they are."

Jane got exited as she heard the story. "Oh I saw something similar, when I stayed there, in the same room, I saw myself, very far in the future though, I was very, very old, and I was with a friend, here in Howth, when suddenly death approached me. I nearly screamed when I had that dream. Only in my dream, Victoria wasn't queen anymore, and there was a fire or something in City Centre, at the GPO building in Dublin. I feel like something is going to happen there, but a very long time from now. I also remember the number 16 reappearing in my dream." Jane thought for a moment, could the ghost allow us to see the future? What was the point of it? I mean if you know how you die, is there a point in knowing the date of your death, you can't prevent your death, you just know that's how it is going to happen. Is there a point to knowing how it happens if you can do nothing about it?" Jane thought about all this.

Eamon got cold, very cold, but spoke "As you know, my family didn't always have money and the castle wasn't always ours. I came to live there when I was four years old, after my grandfather died. He had lived there before us, my parents, my brother and I, that is. Thing is, my parents put me in that very same room and my brother was in the next room, the one that Jane is currently staying in. My brother loved reading stories to me and scaring me before I would go to bed. I had nightmares for years, but thought they were just my brother's stories, until my family decided to put visitors there and change me to another room. The visitors would hear noises or have strange dreams, or hear the screech of death, not everyone could bare it. Priests came, tried to do exorcisms and everything, they even bought images of Christ and our blessed mother and put them throughout the castle, you know, Heath you were asking about the small painting of Christ above your bed? There was a relief of a wooden boat there, but it was a relief of a boat that shipwrecked when one of my ancestors was trying to reach America and when the village priest came and I told him the story about the shipwreck, he told me to get rid of it. It was a gorgeous wood carving, but I gave it as a gift to my old friend Dolly. In the end nothing worked. We got rid of the boat on the wall and the dreams and screeches kept happening. I reckoned time passed and I got used to living in a haunted house but I get lonely and I can't sell the castle as all of Ireland knows about the spirit. Nobody would buy it and besides, it is a bit far from Dublin City Centre, isn't it? At any rate, I have upset myself now. O'Dell, do continue, what have you discovered?"

"Tonight, something happens tonight. Heath, take note, it's past eleven and I am tired, but I will say this, you will wake up the earliest of all of us tomorrow, you all need to stay here for the night, the rain hasn't stopped, and besides, I already have your beds ready, I knew all three of you were going to stay here for the night, because when I stayed in the grey room I saw tonight's events unfold exactly as they are. I saw the rain and you, Heath, whom I have never met and Jane, I saw your violet dress and your black coat in my vision. We will be packed like sardines tonight but you can take the train to Dublin City Centre tomorrow morning. Remember Heath needs to show his art in Marion Square and it is important he goes. Back to my story, though and Heath, listen well: I repeat, I had a dream as well when I stayed in that room and I know I won't wake up tomorrow, I have also seen my own funeral, I'm not scared. I am seventy and it is my time to go."

"Nonsense, O'Dell, you seem in perfect health" said Heath.

"I've heart problems, I think. I don't feel wonderful, from time to time. I repeat, I am not scared, but I know I'm not waking up tomorrow. In my dreams I saw myself reunited with my loved ones, what greater pleasure could there be for an old man?"

This statement frightened everyone except O'Dell, nobody could speak a word after that, but it was late and they all decided to go to bed anyway.

It was true, though, Heath was the first to wake up and O'Dell had died in his sleep. It was a shocking moment for Heath, not only finding O 'Dell dead, but, the way he said it would happen. Beside his body, though, he found a note, which seemed to have been written the night before. The note read:

Dear friends:

First of all, please do not be sad for my death, I lived to my seventieth birthday and that's long enough for me. I was a very happy man in life, so no need for tears, my wife is waiting for me in heaven now, and...

The note stops there, as there was nothing else written in it. A Garda did come to investigate, however, just in case of murder or whatever but he found nothing suspicious and as he asked questions, which everyone was happy to answer, he came to the realization that O'Dell had no known enemies, and for the most part, people liked him dearly. Not only that, but Martin O'Dell was one of the most respected men in Howth. You know the people that absolutely everybody likes and nobody can say anything bad about at all, well that was our friend from Limerick, all of Howth liked the guy a lot. The Garda also said that his note could not have been a suicide note, because there wasn't a suicide. Martin 'O Dell had apparently just stopped breathing. There was a longer examination just to rule out any wrong doing but basically, his heart stopped, really.

In time a funeral was had and people came from as far as Limerick to say a last farewell. O'Dell was buried in the grounds of the Abbey in Howth, as was known that he wanted. There is a headstone that reads "Here Lies Martin O'Dell, born 1795, died 1865"

There was a party on the evening of the funeral. Well not entirely a party but since Martin's family had come in from as far as Limerick, they all decided to get together and have a night to remember him. A big dinner was had and a lot of drink. People sat throughout the house and talked all sorts of stories, like:

"Remember when Old Martin didn't know about the trains and we told him that we were going to Dublin and he had got the horses ready?" said one of his oldest friends.

"Really, he hadn't heard about the trains?" asked another, one of his nephews, who was quite young.

"No, you see, they were very new then and not all of Ireland had heard about them. It was tremendously funny because we told him to show up at the train station, so he did but with horses." Said the wife of his oldest friend. "He said he was ready to go to Dublin and we replied that we were as well but we were going by train. He asked what a train was. We all laughed so hard," continued she.

Similar stories were told throughout the night. Everybody got to know each other a little better then and what was great was the fact that Martin O'Dell had touched everybody's life in a very different way but yet they all remembered a happy man. It is funny, though, as the night carried on, people got louder and louder. There was a woman, must have been a relation of

Martin O'Dell, she might have had quite a lot to drink, or perhaps she is just a noisy person, but she began to say jokes about people and laugh when they would say tragic stories. The poor woman made everyone uncomfortable but some of the stories were funny, although nobody seemed to remember much the next day but that is because at some point, somebody got out the Absinth and everyone started telling stories of Old Martin, even Health told stories and he had only met him once in his life. The good thing about Absinth is the next day, you don't remember a thing and whoever says they do is lying.

Since Martin had everything planned for his passing for years, he had, all this time to think about it. The funeral was not a sad one, as O'Dell would not have liked that. There was a priest, he spoke beautifully about O'Dell and there were flowers and then there was the wild party, but I already mentioned the party.

Life did go on for everybody else, by the way, all of Old Martin's family went back home quite happy that they got to say goodbye to him. See, dear friends, when a young person dies, it is quite sad but when an older person dies, especially an old widower with no children to speak of, it is always expected. But enough sadness for now, let us move to happy events.

Chapter 4

Regarding Heath, though, he did go to the gallery in Marrion Street but not on the day of O'Dell's death, because he didn't think it right proper, to do so. He went afterwards, once things had settled down.

There were days in between the funeral and the visit at Marrion Square that Heath Rochester was creating art and everyone knows that artists have good days when everything goes right, and bad days when by accident you ruin a painting. Rochester had a bit of both. One day, he was finishing a watercolour. He had three next to each other, superb pieces of art, but stupid him, took his coffee into the studio and dropped it on the watercolours. Which were ruined beyond repair. Jane, who was nearby, heard him scream "Damnit!"

"Heath, are you all right?"

"I'm not, look, my coffee has ruined my paintings and even the paper has ripped, I worked so hard on them, I did." Heath was really sad.

"Well it's not the end of everything. You can make new ones."

Heath was in no mood to argue but Jane could see he was upset. He wanted to say "How would you know it's not the end of everything? I need to turn these in tomorrow, now I've nothing to show.' But he was calm, very angry, but calm and he said, "You are absolutely right, it can be fixed." You know those moments when something tragic happens, like a painting being ruined and someone tries to help, but they are only making you more upset? That is what Heath was going through. Heath Rochester was a great man, but he had a flaw. When he was upset he would say horrible things to the wrong person, and the wrong person to be upset with, was Jane. Heath knew he could not say anything rude to Jane, in spite of the fact that on other occasions he would have, although she had nothing to do with him spilling coffee on his paintings. This time he kept quiet, but she could see that he was visibly upset.

Jane was right, though, it was not the end of all things. Sometimes with art, things that you spend a very long time at are discarded as being "too perfect" and things that you spend a half hour at and in a bad mood at that, people love and are willing to pay good money for. Heath Rochester learned that lesson in time, and even though lessons can cause heartache, they become valuable to us. The coffee accident, although it did ruin some superb paintings, made Heath rush and since it was going dark and the next day he would meet very important people in Marion Square, he had one choice, which was to produce as quick as possible, paintings which went as follows:

Painting#1: A seascape, with a sunset, but Heath got the lights and shadows all wrong, so nothing made sense. He was nervous and angry, so he paid little attention to where the light was coming from and this where the shadow would be. That painting is a great one because the sun is setting on one part and the light is hitting the boat on the opposite part, with an unexplained shadow at the bottom, making everything technically wrong, but in time these mistakes were what made Heath Rochester famous.

Painting #2: A landscape with people in it, but things like someone's arm wasn't painted because he forgot to do so and a dog in the foreground was left unfinished. That painting was in time seen as the greatest thing since sliced bread.

Painting the last: The Liffey River, which by the bye would have been superb, had he finished it, but at this time he had painted so much, he was exhausted, so he left it almost as a cartoon, one could say, that done, Heath R. took his things off, went to bed and slept like a baby.

The next day was his big event in Dublin, meeting the fancy people. Heath woke up later than he should have, but he got dressed rather quickly and went downstairs for breakfast and nobody noticed he was tardy.

Heath's trip to Marion Square went well. Jane and Eamon LeFroy and the painter went on the train to city centre and from there, they walked to Marrion Square. It snowed that day, and you should see the snow in Dublin, it's just gorgeous. The whole of Dublin was covered in beautiful, white powder, the parks and gardens looked like a winter wonderland. So, our three friends walked across the Ha'Penny, and stopped to look at the Liffey River as snow fell on it you could almost see the water freeze. The snow falling on all the buildings in the city was a gorgeous sight. The way the snow covered the brick buildings, it made them look like something out of a fairy tale.

For those not familiar with Marrion Street, it is mostly a residential area with wonderful, Georgian houses and very few businesses, hardly any businesses, actually. But there is an art collector that can be found there and he exhibits other peoples' work, as well as his own. The house looks like a private residence from the outside but all the neighbors know that if you want to buy art, this one particular house, is the place to go.

There were our three friends, waiting for the art collector on Marrion Street West at this one gorgeous, Georgian house. They looked around at all the art on the walls, when a tall man walked in. "Ah, Heath from England, is it?" said the man. "LeFroy told me all about you and your paintings. I recognize you, due to your dark hair."

Heath shook his hand. "Yes, thank you, I am the artist, yes. I brought some samples of my work, most though, is photographs of my paintings that I have in York. But I have some watercolours and sketches as well. I do mostly oil landscapes, but I haven't got my oils with me and watercolours will do." Said Heath nervously as the tall man inspected his paintings. Heath was going to tell the tall man about his ruined watercolours but Eamon had advised him earlier not to, for this man in particular likes his artists to not expose any flaws. You see, dear friends, there are two types of art lovers, those that don't want to know when an artist has made a mistake such as spill coffee all over there art (such as the case of the tall man) or those that do and that love hearing stories from artists. This one particular man was not very chatty and could not be bothered with too many stories about how the art was created.

"Hmm, where is this?" said the tall man, holding a painting of a castle that he was examining.

"It's a Norman Castle, close to York, I am from York and this is not that far from my home, sir."

"Oh for an instant I reckoned it was Clongriffin Castle."

"Well both of them are Norman Castles, aren't they? I guess Norman Architecture, thing about it is, it's all quite similar, in a way, isn't it? It is all very imposing. I suppose the idea of the Normans was to make you feel as if you have really been conquered." Said Heath Rochester with a smile.

"I hadn't thought about it, but I suppose you are right. But tell me, I see two mistakes on it, first of all, the tree in the foreground, if you think about it, it is illogically big and second, the grass near the tree, where on earth did you find such green pigments? I find the green almost not natural, some of my clients might not be pleased with it, they would find these two mistakes to be too shocking and however, I doubt they are mistakes. Thing is, I think you made these errors on purpose, first of all, I think the story is not that this is a castle near York, but that there is an enormous tree, and behind it, there is what could be a castle, so, you are thus, telling us the story of a very big tree, as for the green grass, I think you chose to shock the viewer by making unnaturally green grass. I had a teacher, ages ago, she called it Poison Green and that is what you have done, instead of it being calm and soothing, we are frightened by such colours, as if the castle were perhaps scary in a way, the garden with the massive tree and the poison green, my word." The tall man was very dramatic, he loved exaggerating everything, so he did.

"You do not find it to your satisfaction then?"

"Nonsense, I love it. There is an Italian man I happen to know that will be thrilled with this painting, what else have you?" He glanced at the rest of the paintings "hmm, some sheep at sunset. I love this one; you used sepias on this one did you not? Oh and a small watercolour of a lake, people like miniatures these days, I am sure you could produce more if asked. Oh, I recognize this, it is here in Dublin, and my word, you captured the urban landscape perfectly." The urban landscape the tall man was referring to was the Liffey River scene that Heath painted the previous night, when he was tremendously tired.

The tall man was very pleased with Heath's work, he decided to have five of his paintings, which is just as well, for Heath hadn't brought much more than five paintings with him. The agreement was, five for now and were they, with luck to sell, then more were to be fetched later, but were they to not sell, then the tall man would keep these for his private collection. Heath could not have been a happier man, so off he went, after saying goodbye to the tall art collector, down to a nearby pub with his two friends to celebrate; not only that the tall man would keep five paintings, but that he seemed to have overlooked the badly done watercolours. See the art world was changing then, old people wanted something classical, either about a biblical scene or a historic one, etc, but young people were bored with perfection, and liked imperfect paintings because we live in an imperfect world, so there was no need to have things done flawless, and Heath was exactly the man the new, young professionals wanted. His art was not always accurate, but it was pretty, it was very colourful and the people of Dublin loved that, because it was a contrast to the grey skies of Ireland.

Heath, thanks to the promotion of this tall man, would become the biggest sensation in Dublin.

Heath and his friends were at the pub having drinks, watching the snow out the window, they were all smiling.

"Well done, you" said Jane. She was happy because she felt that Heath was going to become a famous artist and this was his first step towards that.

"A toast to Mr. Rochester, the artist." Said LeFroy with a smile. Everybody raised their glass to Rochester. "So, I've a question. Your artistic name, what is it going to be?" continued Eamon. He was wondering, was it going to be Heath, or Rochester, or H.R. or something else? Artists can even invent a name for themselves, can't they?

Heath thought for a minute, he didn't like the sound of H.R. it was too empty, no feeling to a name like that, he reckoned. When he was an art student he signed his paintings as Rochester, or H. Rochester, but as he got more experience he began signing them as Heath or H, so he said "I will remain being Heath." Everyone was pleased with that answer. There is more to the story, though. When Heath was a student there was already another Mr.

Rochester and in the art world you can't have two people with the same name, it's not proper, so that is why Heath decided to keep signing his art with the name, Heath.

Jane was a very sociable woman and not shy at all, so she got up and started telling other people at the pub that she was sat with a man that would one day be a famous artist. People replied things like "my word" or "oh, is that so?" Heath got embarrassed when folks approached him and said things like "So, an artist, is it?" Fellows asked about his art and what style he painted. Some people said that they knew other artists as well, but then people would say names of artists and ask if Heath knew them and then he had to say that he sadly didn't. You see, Heath knew very few artists back then, none of which were famous.

As everybody was talking about Heath the artist and about how his meeting had gone with the tall man, Rochester realized that he did not know his name and that it was very rude indeed to not know the name of the person promoting your art.

"Dolly" Said LeFroy.

"That's Dolly?"

"Yes indeed, my good friend Dolly, he was at my castle once when all the paintings fell from the walls, he has witnessed the spirit first hand. His name is Adolph but he prefers to be called Dolly." Continued Eamon.

Heath R. sat there a bit puzzled, He had heard the name of Dolly being mentioned but somehow pictured the person to be remarkably different and not at all a very tall man, but he did agree that if your name were Adolph that Dolly would do.

As everyone was talking in the pub, they noticed that it had stopped snowing. Everybody was happy because now they could leave and go about there activities. Jane was especially happy, but then everything made her happy. Heath loved the fact that she was so entirely cheerful. Let me describe Heath Rochester's feelings for Jane:

Rochester, like all good artists was a sensitive man. But he had struggles in life, so he knew that the right woman for him would have to be a kind, friendly one, preferably religious, although what religion she practiced was of no consequence. You see he was a Christian, and supposing Jane had been an atheist, then they would just argue all the time, so he was pleased to know that she was a

Catholic. Heath also liked her youth, she was barely twenty, and acted fifteen, but Heath really liked that, because it meant that she was in no hurry to grow up, although he knew she was not stupid, because she would say remarkably intelligent things at times. But then she could be childish as well. Jane was pretty, but not an astonishing beauty, and Heath knew that he was more handsome than she was pretty, but her friendliness, and kind soul made up for her looks. And, see, she was not remotely plain, she was actually pretty, just not VERY pretty, whereas Heath Rochester carried himself like an aristocrat, and sometimes acted like one. At the end of the day, Heath thought "there is no better woman on earth for me than sweet Jane."

After they left the pub and went back to LeFroy's Castle that had recently been covered in snow, Heath went to his room where he was contemplating his life as an artist. He thought of many things, first of all, how lucky he was that an art collector agreed to show his work to those that might be interested, because for someone to show interest in an artist's work is not easy. Second, he thought of his adventures here in Ireland, but he also thought it time to go home for now, although he did not want to. He had only just arrived and his adventures in Ireland (though many) had only just begun, although he had a lot to tell his parents and siblings when he got home. He was starting to realize that he was in love with Jane, even though they had just met. Heath had realized this one thing above everything else, that he would think about Jane every second of the day. When she was away he would wonder where she had gone, and when she spoke with someone and smiled, well he loved that smile. He could not leave her without saying what he felt about her. Heath lied in bed that night, all these thoughts going in his mind, and more. You know those nights when you are in bed and one voice tells you "time to leave Clongriffin Castle" and the other voice says "no, it's to early, there's more adventures ahead". That's the sort of night that Heath had. In the end he decided to just write to his family back in England and tell them that he had decided to stay longer in the castle.

Jane also thought all night long. She thought of Heath. She also thought of the Ghost in Clongriffin Castle for she knew for certain now that it allowed you to see the day of your death and that for some reason it seems to only haunt the grey room. The question was, who was this spirit and why was it specifically in that room? She also wondered if the ghost, or whatever it was, could show you pleasant things, like the day of your wedding, or an image of your children, or the houses you would own in the future, that sort of thing. Imagine, if you know what's going to happen in the future, then you are well prepared for it. Mr. 'O Dell was very well prepared for his death because he had seen it in a dream all those years ago, and he believed his dream to be a vision. Jane remembered that when she had stayed in the grey room before, just like old O'Dell, and like Heath, she too had seen images of her death, although she knew it was many years from now. But she also remembered other dreams that she had in the past in that specific room. She remembered having dreams of things that would later be talked about in the newspapers, or of people that she would meet. She now remembered a specific dream where she was in England, specifically in York, and there was a man who looked astonishingly like Heath, and a voice said, "He will be important in your life". Jane had forgotten that dream, as she had it a long time ago, but she all of a sudden remembered it now, and she thought "goodness me, how could I have forgotten such a dream?" It was obvious that she was to meet Heath and that he was to be an important man in her life.

But Jane also thought all sorts of things about Heath, as she lay in bed. It is not proper for a decent girl to think of a man, when they have just met only a few days ago, but she saw something in him, something magical, in his eyes.

LeFroy, on the other hand, didn't think of anything, really, he fell asleep and woke up the next morning, with instructions to give to the household staff to start breakfast for everyone. Breakfast was ready when everyone woke up. At breakfast, LeFroy said that he had received a letter from a relative of his now deceased friend, O Dell, saying that if Eamon could take care of selling the house, as there was no one to inherit it due to the fact that Martin O'Dell had no children and his siblings in Limerick did not want a house in Dublin. And what's even more so, Howth was too far from Limerick and, besides, a house there would be too expensive to keep, and none of his relations reckoned they could afford it. Old Martin had relations, but they all lived miles away and not one could in reality afford to live in his house. Besides even if they could, most of his relations were his brothers and sisters and they were not of age to move to Howth, as they were now elderly. That said, there was no option but to sell the house, as there was nobody to inherit it to.

Victoria had already been advised about the situation of the O'Dell house, by the time everyone woke up and she was already writing an article for the local newspaper regarding the sale of the house in Howth. Very few people are as efficient as Victoria; really, there is nothing she won't do and everything she puts her mind to is done to perfection.

"So, Eamon, how can I be of service?" asked Heath, eager to help with whatever was asked of him, when he was informed about the sale of the house.

"Well, thing is, the house needs to be left without furniture or any belongings if it is to be sold. I was thinking, do you reckon you and Jane could go and see what things could be brought to the castle, and what stuff could be sold?"

"Neither of us mind, do we, Jane? We can leave this instant, if you like"

"I hope you don't mind. The sooner the better, actually, there will be people wanting to buy the house soon enough, no doubt."

Neither Jane nor Heath minded, besides, it might be fun to go through someone's things, and see what is to be done with what. For this task, Victoria accompanied them. She had a good idea of what was to be done and knew that it would take a while, so she explained Jane and Heath in detail all the chores that had to be completed.

There was more to it, though, in reality, going through Martin's things, that is. You see, Old Martin had not kept his house in top condition in the past few years, so not only did they have to get rid of the furniture, but they would have to give it a bit of maintenance as well in order for the house to sell. O'Dell had good health, save for a heart problem he was not aware of, however, he had noticed that he got more and more tired the last few years. So his house had sadly been neglected.

Victoria had known for some time that the house would go for sale and that everything inside would need to be sold, so she had (with O'Dell's permission) done a list of what would go where, in the event of his death.

The belongings of the house were as so:

Antique furniture, dating as far back as the time of Cromwel,l was to be kept. The same went for the piano.

Clothing was to be given away to those in need. Some families had not recuperated from the famine and were in dire need of clothing, even old clothing. Anything would do. And there was lots of very old clothing, but it's better to wear something that's several decades old, than to wear nothing at all, especially in this cold weather.

Everything in the kitchen was to be divided; half was to be sent to the castle, the other half, to those in need.

Household decorations were divided as well. Those that were antiques were to be kept in the castle, as were newer decorations that everyone knew LeFroy would like. As for the rest, it was also to be given to charity. The subject of a sale was mentioned, but Old Martin was such a kind person, so generous indeed was he, that the thought of someone profiting from his chairs and tables seemed silly, especially when there are those that can't afford food, much less a chair to sit on. And Victoria knew that. So at the end of the day, nothing was to be sold and everything that was not sent to the castle was to be given to charity.

Our group of friends divided the chores: Jane went through things in the kitchen, sorting out pots, pans, knives, forks, etc.

Heath went through Old Martin's clothes, and Victoria sorted out all the furniture. She could not carry any of it, but she at least dusted them.

Heath was looking at O'Dell's clothes, putting them away for charity as he was told. Most of the clothes were what he called old people clothes, meaning it was not antique at all, just out of fashion. A few things were worn before Heath had been born so he thought, perhaps a theatre production would like them for when they do plays that take place a while ago. He asked Victoria about it, but she said: "No, Martin wanted absolutely everything to go for those in need."

Then there was Jane in the kitchen. In her house back in Galway they had a kitchen, but it was a very small one, whereas this kitchen had more pots and pans that she knew what to do with. There was also fine china, which looked very expensive, but she did not know what to do with any of it. She thought: "Do I put things away for the poor, or are they to be sent to the castle?" In reality she made one or two mistakes, sending a few things to the poor, which were to be sent to the castle, but at the end of the day, OK, so some needy families got fine china, the good thing is, they were able to sell what they got and use the money for things they needed.

Not all the finery was by accident sent out to the poor. Many things were sent to the castle, which was great because that way the kitchen staff could use new (or new to them) things to cook with.

As for Victoria, she had mentally separated what was for charity and what was to be taken to the castle ages ago, so now she had it easy. She was also very clever because she knew that she could not carry anything but she knew the neighbours here in Howth and she asked them to help her lift the furniture and send it to the castle. Gather, she did give a few things to those who gladly helped as gifts yet, several pieces were sent to LeFroy Castle in Clongriffin.

Just when everyone thought that they were nearly done deciding what went where they realized the house hand an attic. Not all houses in Ireland have attics, so they were not expecting to find one, but when they went to explore it, they realized that it would take almost an army to explore it well. There was old furniture, hats, old clothes from the 18th and perhaps the 17th century...

Everything was old, there, even letters that were from two centuries ago, some were. Cobwebs filled the room, as did dust and dead insects, it was not a pleasant site.

Our three friends sat patiently, deciding what to do with everything, when Victoria realized, some of these belongings used to be at the castle before. She remembered seeing them there. "I wonder why Mr. LeFroy would leave his things here," said Victoria.

Amongst the many belongings, were an old gun, perhaps used by the LeFroy family and several bullets nearby. The gun was perhaps made in the mid 18th century, even earlier. There was also medicine that appeared to have never been used, articles from newspapers and such. Why would Eamon hide things here, if there was plenty space in the castle, it just did not make sense. Everyone was fascinated about the gun, though, it was of a Baroque design, and was kept in perfect condition. It was obviously an old gun, because technology had progressed in the last two centuries, and this being in the 1860's, people had more sophisticated weapons, whereas a few centuries ago people were still using primitive looking guns.

"Look at this gun I found" said Jane

"Oh my, it's decorated with seashells, how strange," mentioned Heath

Victoria was not impressed. "Listen, some children from the area used to come visit the family of O'Dell all the time, since the O'Dell's never had children, they were more than happy to have as many children over as they could. If any of them saw the gun and thought it to be a toy, it could be very bad. Do hide it" Victoria was nervous when she said this and, in a sense, she was right.

She was spot on, Victoria was, regarding the children. Jane looked out the window and there was a group of youngsters staring at the house, asking if there was going to be any tea today.

"See, I told you, Martin O'Dell always had tea for them at this hour, and his wife always had biscuits ready. She would make them herself, and if she did not have biscuits, she had bread."

That said, the gun was put away in a box and placed on a shelf where nobody would find it. The children from Howth were allowed in the house, though not until the gun was put away. They knew that Old Martin was no longer there, but since they saw people inside they wondered if there might be tea, and there indeed was. No house in Ireland can go without tea, even when trying to sell a house that someone just died in, you still keep the kettle on. You see, this house was always a happy home, one where guests could come in and out as they pleased. The family of O'Dell loved telling stories of the good old days, before the famine. "Life was easier back then" Mrs. O'Dell would say "Everybody was friendly then," she would add. Martin would add how now everybody was more conservative and how before people were more confident, more open minded, that is according the O'Dell household. It was true, though, life does change and hardships did indeed make people more conservative.

That night, they all went to the castle for supper, and asked Eamon about his belongings in the attic at the O Dell house. LeFroy did not give a straightforward answer, but then again, he never did. He just said he got tired of seeing the things in the castle, and O'Dell did not mind keeping them. He did explain, however, that some things were best forgotten. The gun, for example, was the one that one of his relatives used it to end his life. He said that his great, great grandfather had shot himself dead one Christmas, many decades before he was born, and someone apparently had kept the gun, although why on earth would they do that was beyond his understanding. Victoria, who had full knowledge about the suicide, was also bewildered about why anyone would keep that weapon. Many times she had wondered why nobody sold it.

As for the medicine, well, most of his family (past and present) had needed some at some point, including his great-grandfather who died at the age of forty-one, and several of his aunts and uncles, which were prone to illness, but there was no point in keeping medicine. Times had changed and scientists were discovering new and more effective ways of curing people, so all the old bottles were of little use, and were thus tossed out. See in the 18th century, and the first half of the 19th century, knowledge of medicine was in it's early years, so what was kept in this box, by the 1860's was considered outdated, so there was no point in keeping old stuff that by now served no purpose.

Regarding the newspaper articles, they just mentioned events from his family, christenings, funerals, weddings, etc. Even Eamon's father's christening gown was nearby, and a few wedding dresses, including his mother's, and his auntie's. Some of the clothes, like baby gowns were kept, for memory sake, but the wedding dress that Eamon's mother wore was thrown out, because Eamon Lefroy had no wife and would thus have no children, and nobody would want to be married in an old dress from the times of King George. Little did Eamon know that one-day people would collect Georgian dresses and put them in museums, especially wedding dresses. They now have a certain value, where, people feel they tell a story, and if that story took place a long time ago, and if it was a romantic one at that, as some weddings tend to be, then people pay more because they go "here is such a dress with a very lovely story to it." The dress that Eamon's mother wore on her wedding day was just tossed out and lost and one day there was no memory of it.

Jane did see the dress one last time, though. She tried wearing it, but there was no point to it, as the dress was made for a much thinner person. "Look cousin, everything is so delicate, even the buttons. Is it Chinese silk?" But, oh how she wanted that wedding dress. There were several reasons why she could not have it, though. First of all, it was made during the reign of Mad King George, and fashion had changed so much since then, and if Jane were to have worn it, she would have looked absurd. Second, Eamon's mother was both shorter and thinner than Jane, so there was no way she could fit in that tiny dress, although she did love looking at it.

Our friend Jane imagined herself in her wedding, wearing a dress as beautiful as this. She always thought of her wedding, married to a kind man, the wedding would be in the prettiest setting ever, perhaps a castle or some great, country house, and all her friends and family would be there.

"Remember, dearest Jane, our great-grandmother made clothes. She was so good at dress-making that all the ladies in Dublin would go to her. When my mother got married, she made the dress for her from materials a man would bring from Paris." Said Eamon.

Jane had heard the story a million times, but she loved hearing it. Jane could not make dresses, you see. She once tried making a scarf, but it didn't go as planned. Like I mentioned, Jane is a big woman, and when she sat down to make the scarf, she realized she had done one for a person half her size. Then she tried making a purse. It was supposed to be in the shape of a pineapple, but it didn't come out the way she wanted at all. Just the same she felt happy that there was a dress maker in the family, once upon a time, and that people admired her work, even though they did not know what to do with any of it. Jane was a romantic in many ways, as she looked at the dress she remembered stories of their great-grandmother. See, Dublin was a smaller place then, and there were fewer places to buy gowns and such, so a good seamstress could make good money and she was the best in Dublin once, her and Eamon's great-grandmother was. It was an honour to be a descendant of such a wonderful person.

Eamon could not decide what to do with all the other things though. Some things were important but others were not. Here is the scenario, the castle of LeFroy was, as you know, filled with antiques, but the O'Dell family had a house full of things that were in some ways just as old or valuable. But they did not fit in the castle, and since Old Martin and wife had come from Limerick with no belongings, Eamon had thought it right to let the O'Dell's have quite a lot of furniture. I must say, though, I have now bored the reader by telling stories about random things that were found I should now move on. But before there is one last thing to mention. See neither Jane nor our English friend, Heath, had thought of the most important thing of all, the money. Allow me to paint a picture for you, as it were:

A piece of furniture, say a buffet, has been in the LeFroy family for three centuries, however, there are plenty of pieces of furniture just like it, so taking it from Howth to the castle in Clongriffin costs money and there is a risk of the furniture being damaged. Eamon stressed about the idea of selling the furniture, vs keeping it. There was a lot to consider, like the fact that Ireland had gone through tough times recently, so very few people had enough money to pay for a tremendously expensive piece of furniture. So were he to sell it, it would have to be for a fraction of what it was worth, but were he to keep it, he would have to pay people to send it to the castle, and the road was bumpy, so the risk of things not getting to the castle in prime condition was a real one. Poor Eamon LeFroy did not sleep well at all. He told everyone to bring the furniture to the castle (what was worth keeping) but he wasn't sure it was the right idea.

Chapter 5

The next few days Heath went to the garden outside the castle to paint. He found a new technique, which was to do quick paintings, with swift brush strokes. He realized that people liked his new technique, whereas before he would spend days, even months at a single painting and he noticed that people did not like them as much, yet people adored his new ones. See, times were changing and not everyone wanted perfect art. There was a new, younger audience that wanted paintings that you create within hours, at most a day or two, as opposed to what was full of detail and elaborately done. Funny, Heath remembered when he was in the Art Academy, and if anyone has ever been to one, the art professors are very strict and do not allow for any creativity. Heath Rochester is very creative but his technique is not the best in the world. Our friend Heath remembered how when he was in the Art Academy, his professors would give him tasks, like painting something from Greek Mythology, or a scene from the life of a certain saint, but Heath felt that those subjects had been done over again for hundreds of years, and that the younger art market wanted something new, original and that wasn't a painting of Apollo, painted for the thousandth time. Dolly came over a time or two to see Heath's progress and he chatted with Heath about his swift, entirely non-perfect paintings and how he would find clients to purchase them, which happened indeed.

Dolly knew the right people. There was, for example, a couple that rented lodgings for visitors in Dublin City that bought several of Heath's paintings through Dolly's help. There was also a woman that lived towards Wicklow who put Heath's art throughout her house. Some people wanted art for a certain room or as a gift to friends for a Christening. Heath felt like an angel had come down from heaven and had come to tell all of Ireland about his art.

Anyway, there was Heath in the garden painting one day when he remembered his professors and how they would not allow his creativity to blossom. Now his creativity was finally flowing and people loved what he did.

Jane loved observing, as Heath would paint. She would put on her prettiest dresses and look at him, as he would create his art. "Pray, tell, what medium are you using now?" she would ask

"Ah, I asked Eamon the other day, where I could buy art supplies, and he pointed at a place in Dublin, so I took the morning train over and found what I needed, he is so kind, isn't he? I got everything I need to do oil paintings. You see, when I was an art student back in York, getting art supplies was a challenge. I pretty much had to make everything. However, now there are all these new art supplies stores that used to not exist." What Heath said was very true. You see, about fifteen years ago, when Heath started painting, art supply stores were tremendously hard to find, so he had to make absolutely everything himself, meaning he had to do the paints, the brushes, physically construct the canvas himself, etc. Now times had advanced and more and more people fancied taking up art since there were more art supply stores.

"Oh, you are working in oils, are you? I wish I could paint, but I was thinking you should do a portrait of me, I would pay for it." Heath was good at landscapes but not so good at drawing people, but he could not say no to sweet Jane, so he got out a new canvas.

"Sit there if you like, on the bench by the tree." Jane had on her red and black dress today, with her black bonnet she loved so much. Heath started with the sketch and remembered to include the bench and the tall tree. After the sketch he allowed her to relax and take refreshment while he painted the background. There were some grey skies, which he painted, as well as the garden. "It looks like it might rain," he thought.

Jane came back when Heath was done painting the background, and sat while he painted her in her red dress. "Oh it's getting rather cold," said Jane, the muse.

"It will only be a few minutes, then we can go inside." Said Heath with a smile. He continued painting. "Wait, I just need to put in some highlights."

When the painting was done, Jane got up. "Ah, wow, let us show Eamon, I am in love with it." Eamon saw the painting and Heath was paid very handsomely for it. Heath Rochester was in the library when the painting was shown to him; Eamon LeFroy had just received a letter from his auntie and uncle, Jane's parents.

"Jane, I have news from Galway."

"Oh, if its mammy, do tell her I am having too much fun, I can't go back home. I just sat for a portrait, besides, O'Dell's house has not sold yet and I need to help with that. I did promise Victoria I would help, what's more, if I go back to mammy she will only sermon me about some thing or another and I've no time for sermons."

"Oh dear Jane, they just worry about you, is all, and yes, they would like for you to go back, not for your sake, but because your parents just worry."

"Nonsense, I will write to them this instant and tell them that I find myself perfectly well. I can't tolerate Galway. Society is tremendously boring there, besides, there is not much to do-- no gambling, no balls, no plays to see,

Clongriffin is much more fun, really. Not only that, but, see, you don't know Galway like I do. It's a lovely place, it's my home, it's where I am from, but people there are more conservative than I am, I get frustrated there at times."

"See I disagree, I find Galway to be fascinating. Heath, you have been quiet, any words on the subject?"

"I wouldn't know, I have never gone further west than Marion Square, really. On that note, I should write to my parents and siblings as well, they would be worried, but when it comes to tremendously conservative people, Jane might be right. Where I come from not everybody agrees with my point of view. Jane, you and I are similar in that aspect, we are forward thinking people."

"Thank you, and see I get frustrated by a lot of things, like the fact that as a woman I have no rights. All men want is for us to look pretty and not do anything. If I had my way, I would write travel books. "

"You write?" asked her cousin. He had never seen her write a word in his life, but that is because Jane is the sort of person that can only write when nobody is around. She finds that her creativity comes when she is alone. Jane has a secret diary and a few short stories and poems about this and that, but beneath all her flirting and putting on fancy outfits, she is insecure, and her writing is very personal, so were people to read her work, she would blush. She did have a dream, though, which was to write travel books and obviously to travel the world and write about her adventures.

"I do write" she answered her cousin.

That night while Jane wrote her letters to her family in as she put it "boring Galway", Heath wrote to his family.

Dear Parents:

You will not believe the adventures I have had. I found my way to some fishing village and there is a castle not far from it, actually, full of antiques and everything. The castle goes back to the Norman period and the antiques, many of them are from the Tudor period, however the owner, his family had traveled the world, so there's loads of stuff from other countries. We went to Howth, which is the name of the village. It rhymes with "both". Anyway it is not far at all from the castle called Clongriffin, the villagers also call it LeFroy Castle. Anyway, this nice old man passed on, a good friend of the owner of the castle, a Mr. LeFroy, though he insists I call him by his first name, Eamon, but I always pronounce his name all wrong, as it is not a familiar one to me. I don't think there are any Eamon's in York. I can never get his name right. By the bye, he has got the loveliest cousin, Jane. The day I met her she had this gorgeous satin dress, entirely red, she looked like a vision, like some sort of angel, really. She has no idea how much I think about her and I rather feel as if a witch has possessed me for I cannot stop thinking about her. Regardless, I have agreed to help with the selling of the house of the man that died, will write soon.

Your son, Heath R.

Heath got a reply soon enough, but his parents only asked about Jane and if he was actually in love with her, to which he replied that he was. He was astonished at how quick the reply was from his family. He was under the impression that post from England took ages, but the letter from his parents and siblings came much quicker than he ever imagined. Heath thought of the speed in which letters arrived by then, and how incredible it would be if messages could be received within an instant. He thought "imagine if you could write to anyone in the world, regardless of where they were and they would receive your message straight away?" He thought that before 1900 someone was bound to invent a machine that could do that. The telegraph was in a sense that, however, Heath always felt that something could be improved on a telegraph... well Heath was always thinking about this and that, but his thoughts often times bored others when he spoke his mind, so he kept his thoughts to himself, for the most part.

After Rochester answered the letter that he had recieved he put his clothes on and went downstairs. He was happy because the night before he dreamed about York. Heath Rochester had a strange idea about being a North Englishman. He thought of people from the south as barbarians, really. He even went so far as to say once that people from the north were prettier people and far more civilized, so for him, there was nothing better than to be a northerner, and when he dreamed of York, de dreamed of the place with pride. I must add as well that so far as Heath was concerned, being a Northerner was so great that he reckoned the North of England must have been created by Jesus himself. Not everybody shared his point of view but just the same Heath loved

York and thought it superior to any place in southern England.

It was a cold morning, Eamon was reading with Jane by his side, as they were discussing her trip back to Galway. Heath had gone out for a walk since early in the morning and was not around. Jane finally had a chance to tell Eamon LeFroy that she was starting to feel something for Heath.

"Does he speak to you about me, when you are alone?" she asked

"All the time. All I hear is Jane this and Jane that. You wore a red dress once and he was quite impressed by it." Eamon was going to continue when Heath walked in.

"You won't believe it. In spite of the cold and rain I found some flowers. They are starting to bloom, Jane, you must go to the garden with me. I did a painting of them, look." Heath showed the painting to Jane and Eamon.

"Oh I love flowers. Do sit, I am nearly done with my coffee, can we go after I am done?" asked Jane with a big smile.

"Oh please, I shall have some myself."

A staff member brought the coffee and then Heath and Jane went to see the flowers. Eamon needed to go back inside the castle so he did not accompany them this time.

"Daffodils; they came early this year, Jane." said Heath as they walked in the garden. "I need to go back to England to see my parents soon. I can't convince you to come with me, can I?" I have a house in York. Not as big as this but it hasn't any ghosts. No premonitions, no nightmares about death, but you must meet my family, it is a large one, both my family and my house. I have many brothers and sisters, and I know that although you aren't fond of England, because the English are too stiff, as you once mentioned but my family would welcome you. Thing is, I can't stop thinking about you. I know, it's not Ireland, but please visit."

It is a truth universally acknowledged that single women aren't supposed to travel alone, much less with an unmarried man, for it might cause a scandal, but Jane was dying to go. "Let me think about it" she said, with a smile. See, Jane couldn't say 'yes I will go" because of what her cousin might think. Thing is, she knew Eamon well and he might think that were her cousin to be seen with a man that she was not yet engaged to it would be her ruin. On the one hand he was right, leFroy was, for proper Irish girls don't travel with men that they aren't engaged to, much less if they have to stay at a hotel for a night or two. What would people say?

They were speaking, silently when LeFroy approached them. He had apparently forgotten something and came back when he saw his cousin and his artist friend. "Oh cousin, you won't believe it, Heath needs to go back to England and has invited me to go with him, imagine, York." You could see her eyes shine bright when she said those very words.

"I think you would like York. You read a lot and you like history and, you know what, Jane, there's many castles there and abbeys and all of them are haunted. I think you would enjoy a trip there," said Eamon.

The rest of the day was spent discussing the trip. Heath told them all about things to do there, and about his large family, and how they had been settled there since longer than he knew, etc. They talked about all the castles worth seeing, and the shambles, and nearby ruins and things. Jane's imagination went wild. She especially loved hearing about York

Minster, and the stories about how it was built and who is buried there, and so on. She also wondered if there were ghosts there. Heath told Jane how the current York Minster was done in a style called Perpendicular Style and how if you look at the ceiling, it was like looking at a lace gown. People in York say that the Perpendicular ceiling was similar to the fabrics that people used in the Middle Ages. Jane imagined herself a queen back then, in the 1400's wearing lace from head to toe and with a knight fighting other people for her love. She also imagined herself to be the Faerie Queene except, unlike in the books, she imagined all sorts of terrible things like her fighting demons and dragons and a haunted, dark forest where a dashing prince with brown eyes would come rescue her.

That night, as the three were sitting near the fire, dozing off, Jane realized she was nearly done with her book and would need another one for her trip. "Cousin, I'm going to the library, I need to see what book to take."

Off she went and while she was away, Eamon and Heath talked about her trip, and how she would be well looked after. Eamon would have loved to go as well but, like always, he said he had business to take care of. Pretty soon, though, Jane re-entered.

"I found the perfect book: Fanny Hill."

"Fanny Hill? Yes, one of my favorites" said Eamon with joy. Everybody loves the story of Fanny Hill, a woman of pleasure.

"Well I would love to hear about it, but I'm tired," Commented Heath. And off he went to bed. Heath was very tired, it was late in the evening and he had blood shot eyes.

That night, Heath had another strange dream. This was to be his last, though. In his dream he saw a man by the name of Neill who had died a violent death in this room, but he also saw something else. He couldn't tell if it was another man or a group of people in the room. There was something like a cloud in the room and he could see what seemed to be another person or group of people but he knew not how many. Neil was dressed like people did in the late 1700's, he was sat in this very room and he shot himself.

The next morning, Heath asked his friend who Neill was "My great, great grandfather, why? What have you found out about him?"

"He died in my room, didn't he? And most violently so... He is the man you were telling us about, is he not? You know, your great-great grandfather that shot himself. He is without a doubt the ghost that for some reason warns us about our own death. Jane and I were talking about him, she wondered why you can only see the day of your death and why only in that room. Jane asked why the ghost wouldn't show you your wedding day, or the day you buy a house, or your future children, etc. I think your great-great grandfather, Neil, his soul is in torment for ending his life in the grey room and he doesn't want anybody to suffer the same fate as him, am I right?"

"He committed suicide there, and after he died, they found a letter, saying that he would come back t haunt us. It was worse than that, actually. My great-great grandfather, Neil, he shot himself at Christmas. He was an alcoholic, and a most violent one at that. He never treated his wife kindly, my great, great grandmother. While Neill lived his wife and children suffered a great deal but after he died, certain things started happening. My great grandfather died shortly thereafter, of an illness. Nothing alarming except for the fact that he was quite young. My grandfather inherited the castle, but he lived alone for the most part. He is the one that decided that the grey room should look more uplifting. It was too dark and perhaps a change in colour would brighten things up. Anyway, about him, I mean he had my grandmother with him, but long story short, I doubt it was an ideal marriage. My grandfather was not violent in the sense that he never hit anybody, however he did get angry quite frequently. He had a violent, grumpy temper and my poor grandmother suffered a great deal because of it. I remember things like, well as you know, there are no shops here so if they needed anything they needed to go to Dublin. And the trains did not exist then, so it happened more than once that when they were on their way back and my grandmother would say "Oh I forgot this or that" my grandfather would get tremendously angry. Even with Jane, we once went to Howth to see the deer, and Jane was a child and had a fall and cried, as is normal for a child. Well, grandfather, God bless him, got tremendously angry at Jane for falling and for crying. I remember it well, we were all scared.

When my father inherited the castle, he and mother actually had a normal life, besides the nightmares, and they both died the way great-great grandfather Neil predicted. My mother was a sociable person, always entertaining people. When they lived here in the castle they had huge balls and parties of all sorts and everyone in Howth was invited. My father was less sociable, he was prone to being stern and when he tried to make a joke, he would get it wrong and then would have to explain it. Nobody found that funny, really, but bless his cotton socks, he tried telling jokes.

When I met O'Dell, I tried convincing him to get rid of any evidence that Neil had ever lived. There is a book on the family history that one of my aunties put together. She is still alive, though very old. You would love her, such an extravagant woman, reminds me of Mrs Havisham, really. You had it in your hand when you went to the attic, her book, you just did not know what it was."

"Well that solves that problem. Now I know perfectly well who the ghost is. It's Neill, your ancestor. Now, how do we get him to stop haunting whoever stays in the room, and how do we know why he killed himself, and who was the man in the room with him? I've a million questions, I don't know where to start," said Heath. Heath Rochester's head was spinning. He had heard about a suicide or murder in the room he lived in, then of a man that died shortly thereafter, of an eccentric woman and of all sorts of things. He needed to relax, maybe see if Victoria could get him a soda or a brandy, or brandy with soda, or whatever, really.

"If you need to know, Neill, had five mistresses that we know of, plus he never treated his wife with any respect, and was an alcoholic. He would get enormously depressed when he drunk and one day he grabbed the gun you saw and he shot himself. Thing is, put yourself in his shoes, imagine you are in this very castle shortly before 1770, your wife hates you, your children can't look at you, and your five mistresses all know that their children they had with you will never inherit the castle. What's more, many of his bastard children have worked here before. One still does. That is why he killed himself. He would spend all his money on loose women and drinking and he was going to lose the castle. I have thought about it before, he was such a tremendous wreck that had he not shot himself, one of his mistresses would have done so. See, back then men were allowed to hit women, now almost nobody does. Anyway, at first everything was fun, then he would get bored of one, treat her horribly and move on to the other one."

Victoria (who was walking in with soda) was a descendant of Neill and his affair with a maid. Her family had stayed in the castle since then. Victoria never saw the suicide, she knew about it, but she never saw it as this was the mid 1860's and she was in her fifty's so she could never had witnessed the event as it happened years before she was born. Victoria looked younger than her age. But I will tell you her secret: she died her hair and used cosmetics to cover up her wrinkles and she was also fond of high heels and walked like a queen, thus looking younger altogether. Eamon also dyed his hair. He had gone grey about a decade ago and hated it and eventually found some dyes to cover up his grey hair.

"Are you sure your great -great grandfather was not murdered?"

"Positive, he did it in front of his friends at a Christmas party."

"That is gruesome. I couldn't imagine anything worse, but hang on a minute, why was everybody in that room that night? It was Christmas, shouldn't they be out at church or having dinner? Didn't you say there were others in the room?" asked Heath.

"He called them to the room, he had been drinking heavily, and made an absolute ass of himself, but he always did. Everybody followed him up to his room, but in hope that he might fall asleep. They started to undress him, but found a gun in his pocket, he grabbed it and right then and there shot himself dead. So, now you know. My cousin, Jane, thinks we should sell the castle. I don't want to torture the future owners with a ghost. I don't know what to do. I would be honored if you could take Jane with you to England while I decide. Don't worry, I don't drink, and I am not a depressive sort, and Victoria has already given the gun to my friend Dolly. He is fond of old guns and he absolutely loved the seashell decoration it has on it. I will be fine, just so you know. The ghost has showed me my death in a dream and it's not for a while now. I just, don't want Jane to be burdened with, well with my having to choose what to do with the castle, and perhaps having to move everything. Besides, she is a happy person, if you remind her of her family's past, it might torment her. We can't ruin her happiness. I would prefer her to go to York with you for a few weeks. I could meet you there, if you like. By the way, this is of utmost importance, what is your address in York? I think that in a week or so I will come visit, if I may?"

"Are you sure you don't want a priest to see the house? And I must warn you; I don't own a castle. I own a big house in York, but it's not a castle. You are free to visit, but I've fourteen siblings. We would be tight, having said that, you are more than welcome to visit. "

"Many priests have come to bless my house from as far as Rome. One said to have fire be put out with fire. I know what he means, but the house is too beautiful to be burnt. See I even had a group of demonologists study the castle. They live in the north. It was about a month before you came. Remember Dolly, the man that buys your art? Dolly is a friend from Dublin, as you well know, well he heard about these people that study demons, they came to the castle and tried to get rid of whatever was haunting the place, but since there is no satanic being in the castle, just a tormented spirit, all their conjuring was for nothing," said Eamon LeFroy.

"But the furniture is even more beautiful than the castle itself. Look, I've an idea. Take the furniture out, put it somewhere else. It is all yours, and after all, the furniture is. Buy another house, maybe not a castle this time, but we are in the 19th century, there are so many gorgeous houses all over Ireland, you would be bound to find one. Move elsewhere, and lock this old castle up. Meet me in York; I will in the meantime entertain your cousin. Does she like nuts? I've a walnut tree, I could show her my nuts, she will love to harvest them."

The plan was agreed upon and Heath and Jane left the following day.

Chapter 6

Jane was welcomed with open arms in the house of Heath's family. All of Heath's siblings were tremendously interested in hearing all about Ireland.

"Tell us about the castle." One would say.

"Is it old, is it scary, is it dark?" another would say, then someone else would go "is it true that Ireland is quite green?" Everybody knows that England is very green, but Ireland is much greener than England, because it rains more. See, English people, when they travel abroad go "my home town is so green" but Irish people go "you don't know what greenery is until you have been to Ireland." England is gorgeous and is very green, but Ireland is far greener.

There were many, many questions, and many stories that everyone wanted to hear about Ireland. The family would stay up by the fire every night to hear the stories. Jane did indeed feel at home, she was afraid at first, that she would not like England, since it is very different to Ireland, and because her family had always said that it was better to be single for ever than to marry someone from England, so she grew up with this idea since she was a girl. But Heath and his family were far kinder to her than she ever dreamed they would be. She liked this family, and they liked her. She also liked the fact that they showed her all the sites in York. She soon grew to love the place, although she thought frequently of Ireland. Jane loved going out for walks as well. Jane's favorite thing of all the sights she had seen though was York Minster. It is quite impressive how such buildings were constructed so many centuries ago. Jane was an optimistic person and that helped her enjoy her journey in York.

Jane loved stories about York Minster and how the central tower once fell in the Middle Ages, or how an Anglo-Saxon king was once baptized there. She also learned how the church was once made out of wood, but was now out of stone, which was great, because stone buildings last longer. Although, having said that, in the year of 1840, the church did catch fire and she wondered if that happened again what the result would be, would they rebuild it or would they put another church in it's place or whatever?

One day, not long after they had arrived in York, Heath took Jane to a nearby town, Whitby, for a picnic where they had tea in the park. For those that don't know Whitby, it is small, there is an abandoned abbey and the wind howls there all the time. The town is charming as well. Jane and Heath walked there, in the town first and then they went to a nearby park for tea and food of all sorts and loads of tea. Heath's family did not join them on this trip, for he asked to be left alone with her.

"Jane, I was wondering, you seem very happy here indeed. Would you, that is, we are both single, and you have seen how I live. It is not glamorous, but it is what I have to offer. Would you love to be my wife? Do say yes." Heath was tremendously nervous, and struggled to say these few words.

"Yes. I was beginning to wonder if you would ever ask."

"I am so glad, what a relief! Had you said no, I don't know what would have become of me."

Heath got down on one knee as he spoke, and put a ring on Jane's finger. The ring was one that had been handed down from his family, and was nothing new or impressive, but Jane did not want anything new and fancy.

Heath's mother, Elizabeth was the first to hear the news upon their return from Whitby. "My son is to be married, and to this beautiful girl, look at you, luv. Oh dearest (to her husband, Henry) Let us tell our friends, and oh Jane, I know a dressmaker, and a cake, you need a cake. Oh my word, how much excitement."

Poor Jane, though, she liked her new mother-in-law, but she was realizing that with her involvement, everyone in the north of England would go to the wedding, and they would have her wear the biggest dress anyone had ever seen, and it would probably end up being in The Queen's House, the wedding would be, down in London or something huge like that, and the thing is, Heath's mother, although she didn't have a tremendous amount of money for something as big as that, she had some money saved in the bank for her children's future and she did want something huge. However Jane had always wanted something small, maybe close friends and family only and nothing beyond that. Jane had dreamed of a wedding in a garden with only the closest of friends around, but she could tell that her new mother-in-law wanted the biggest event ever. Jane also worried if she could get her family over from Ireland for the occasion. She also needed to set a date, have a menu, have bridesmaids, she wanted a white dress, white flowers, perhaps an early morning church service followed by breakfast for the guests. She also wanted her husband to show up in blue, he looked good in the following colours: blue, violet, green and grey, but every time he wore blue she would nearly faint at the sight of him because he would look amazing.

As for what Heath wanted, he didn't care if they got married in York or in Ireland or as far as India, or wherever, really, or if it was in The Queen's House in Greenwich or in his parent's garden, all he wanted was to show up and that's it. Heath was a kind man, sensitive, but he wasn't into weddings, but he knew everybody would help organize it. To be honest, Heath liked weddings as much as people like cockroaches. He tried to avoid them at all cost and whenever he got invited to one he found a reason to not go and would send one of his siblings to represent him. There is a reason behind Heath's hatred of weddings. See, as an artist he had spent years and years painting and selling art when he could. One day, shortly before he left for Ireland, he realized that most of his friends were married and had children and he was still single. But really for years he had avoided weddings because once there people would ask when his turn was to get married so he decided not to go, instead what he did was to save his money and go to Ireland where nobody knew him. Now Heath is back and has brought Jane along with him.

The entire family of Rochester helped with the wedding invitations and everything, so they did. One day, though, as the family was talking about the wedding, after they had gone to see Heath's grandmother, who was in charge of making a white dress for Jane and a blue suit for Heath, there was a knock on the door as they were all together, sat by the fire. One of Heath's sisters got the door.

"A man in an Irish accent has come."

"Oh do let him in, surely it's one of Jane's relations." said Henry, Heath's father. Jane looked puzzled, she hadn't written to her family yet, she had been so busy with flowers and dresses and choosing what to give everyone for breakfast after the ceremony that she plumb forgot to write to her relations in Galway and to her cousin in Dublin and tell them about her wedding.

"Hello, I've come from Ireland, does a Mr. Heath live here?" Heath went to see the man.

"Yes I do."

"Oh grand, I have a message from Clongriffin Castle, I traveled all the way from there. Thing is, tragedy has happened there. LeFroy, I think he went quite mad, really."

"Mad?"

"Well he acted strange when you and Jane left. You see, Victoria, my cousin, she called on me when you left, and she had me help with taking all the furniture and art out of the castle. We were not told why, but were told to do so Dolly came over to help as well. We received a good payment for removing all the furniture, so I was put on a boat to England after that, told where to reach you, and here I am. Now if I am allowed to sit and have refreshment, I have been traveling for ages, I have." The man sat down, and was handed water. Then continued the conversation. "Poor Eamon, I heard he is selling the castle, though, for what little money anybody was willing to give."

"I've a little bit of money," said one of Heath's brothers, a small boy. The boy did not comprehend that a small bit of change in his pocket could not buy a castle, as he was too young to understand the conversation.

Everybody discussed what to do with the castle, they also wanted to talk about the antiques, but Victoria's cousin insisted there was nothing to be done, that they had been sent somewhere, though he knew not where.

"Perhaps I should go see him." Said Jane as they talked.

"Well he is your cousin after all, if he is quite unwell, then you should." said Henry. Jane did go to Ireland.

The trip to Ireland was uneventful the sea was actually much calmer than one expects it to be. Jane arrived in Dublin and took the train to Howth, where Victoria. met her. "Eamon is well, do not worry, it is the castle. We were moving all the antiques, and the grey room caught fire, but nobody was in the room then. I can not explain it, because see, it was a long day, we had taken everything out of the castle, to have it sent some place you will soon find out, and we had come to Howth to have some food and had all left the castle, we were all very hungry. The strange part is, not a single person was in the castle at the time, nor were any candles left on or any lamps of any sort. It was last Sunday, and all the staff was given the day off. We came to the castle, and saw the flames. A man came to investigate, he did a great job at it, and although he found no arsonist, he did find evidence that the fire had started in the Grey room, how they figure these things out is beyond me, but anyway, poor Eamon is in shock."

"What nobody knew yet was: remember when old Martin died, and the antiques they found in the attic? One of them was cursed, we don't know by whom. Legend has it that at some time in the seventeenth century a witch came to Ireland from across the sea, and she stayed at the castle in the very same grey room, but she felt she was not treated kindly so she cursed the place and every object in it. Nobody in Ireland today believes in witches, but what is true is that some of the objects such as mirrors broke without reason, paintings from the entire castle fell from there walls, that happened even until some days before Heath arrived, not every day, but once every couple of years or so. Also, doors would slam and windows would open and close for no reason and knives had been flying through the castle... there was a lengthy investigation and to not bore you, here is what happened, as they say, in a nutshell:

"A woman did come to the castle from abroad in the 1690's and the then-owner was a grumpy man. His children had left and gone to Galway to live for they could not tolerate his foul temper. One of them was Jane's ancestor, so it was no surprise that the house guest was mistreated. She did curse the castle, beginning with the very room she stayed in, and she stormed out and left the castle, never to return, but she left some daggers in the room. The daggers were said to fly through the room without anybody moving them, until one day around 1850, Eamon gave them as a gift to Old Martin. When Old Martin heard about the witch he had them locked in the attic. When he died and everyone went to pack his things, nobody thought anything of the daggers, not even Victoria. She was more worried about the old gun they found than some old knives, so she brought them back to the castle and that is when Eamon began acting like a mad man.

"There was more to the story, though, you see. For generations the family of LeFroy was cursed. At first it was nothing major, just someone having a stroke of bad luck, say, but then things got worse. It got to a point where whatever the LeFroy's tried to do, it would come out wrong. Many family members lost all their money and took to working in the streets, others had businesses that failed and left them in ruin, while others yet felt darkness everywhere they went. One day Eamon's great-great grandfather, Neil ended his life in the room that the witch had cursed. His life had been a disaster from start to finish and it was not going to get any better ever. He did not know of the curse or the witch but he knew that no matter what he did he could not be happy. When Neil died, the power of the curse got weaker. Neil's son (who was now married and with children) died the next year but of sadness, not of a curse, and Neil's grandchild (Eamon's grandfather) grew to be a grumpy man. But the witch's curse could have no power beyond just making him ill tempered. You see, the curse would lose strength when a person would die in pain in the very room that the witch stayed in, and that had happened upon Neil's death-- although it did not go away, it just was not as strong. The witch had also allowed people to see their death because it is what she wanted, for anyone that would stay in that very room to see the day and hour of their death and to not be able to do a thing about it."

Jane arrived to what remained of the castle, and there she saw Eamon, unhurt physically, but mentally quite shaken. "What happened?" Jane asked and that is when she was told about the curse of the daggers.

"Our ancestor, the one that shot himself one Christmas party, decades ago, I don't believe in the supernatural, but there is something you must know, dearest Jane. On the night of his funeral, guests said that they smelled something burning, when asked where the smell came from, it was from his room, the grey room. A lot of strange things happened right there, items showing up in random places, and clocks stopping for no reason, even paintings falling off the shelves. Remember the one painting in that same room the painting of the boat? It fell once, and broke. A man tried to repair it, but could not, so I bought a painting of Christ and put it in that room. Things stopped falling and breaking without reason, I didn't know if it was because I brought a blessed painting into the room or because I gave every cursed object to old Martin to have locked up. But the dreams continued. When it was obvious that the dreams were a prediction of what is to come, after Old Martin died the exact same way he dreamed it when he stayed in the room, it was obvious to me that it had been my great-great grandfather, the one who died there, whose ghost was doing all this. I don't know how the fire started, I may never know, but I have no doubt it was him," said Eamon, only he was wrong about one thing. It wasn't his ancestor that killed himself that caused the terror, it was the witch that cursed the place, and whose curse caused him to run mad and kill himself, but thing is, nobody alive remembered the witch, but how could they? Nobody's memory went that far back. Things were discovered in time, though. Even burned down places leave clues of the past.

Eamon did not then know about the witch, he only knew about his great-great grandfather dying in that very room, but in time the entire truth was found out.

"First of all, I have a lot of questions. I have stayed there, and have seen the date 1916, ever since then that number has appeared multiple times, I think I die then, but no matter, I would be an old lady. Second, where will you live? Are you going to rebuild?"

"My cousin, I can't rebuild this, it is a pile of grey and black rocks now, who wants to buy them? And besides, I have written to Heath, he knows everything I just told you and I am in luck, there is a new house in York, Heath's parents were building it for when either him or one of his siblings would get married, that they could live in this new house. My furniture has already been sent to England," said Eamon.

"I know that house, it's not one house, it's two, across the street from each other, really pretty ones, Heath showed me them the other day." Said Jane in deep thought. Hang on a minute, if you go to York, what will happen to dearest Victoria?" continued she.

Victoria was not at that moment with Jane and Eamon as she thought it right to let them have there privacy, so she had gone off to walk, and was unaware she was being talked about. "Victoria", said Eamon LeFroy, "Remember Dolly in Marion Square? I had some paintings that were worth some money, actually quite a lot of money, and I sold them to him. Every penny I got from selling the paintings went to Victoria for her decades of loyal service to me, she is a wealthy woman and can do whatever she wishes to do with her money."

"And the art dealer in Marion Square, Dolly, does he want to see any more art? Heath has an entire room filled with art that has not sold." Inquired Jane. This was very much true. When Jane was in England, Heath had showed her a room full of art that although was some of his best work it had failed to find a costumer. Dolly was the right man to sell Heath's art.

"Well we have to stay at his place tonight, nobody can stay here, it's all in ruins, the entire castle is. Why don't you ask him?" said Eamon. Just then Victoria appeared. Our three friends went to Marion Square, to where Dolly was waiting for them with open arms. Dolly was a very friendly man who loved company so he had already made dinner for Jane, Eamon and Victoria.

"Eamon, I heard what happened to your castle. Tragedy, isn't it?" Said Dolly at dinner.

"Yes and no. I mean it's sad to see the castle go up in flames, but way I see it, at least none of the furniture was in it, and now I can sell the land. I finally have buyers interested. But listen, thanks for letting us stay here for the night, you are grand." Said Eamon

"Am happy to do so," replied Dolly.

Victoria and Jane went to the kitchen while Dolly and Eamon talked in private after dinner and they chatted about all sorts of things, and Eamon talked to Dolly about a possibility for Heath to show his work somewhere in Dublin. There was a neighborhood, not that far from Dublin Castle that had a place for Heath to exhibit. Dolly the art dealer just needed to see when space would be available.

Dinner was now over and done with as was their chat, and the men joined the women. "Jane, I've good news, I am going to write tomorrow to a man I know, he has a place near Dublin Castle and he can show your friend Heath's work if you like, we just need to see when," Said Dolly the tall man.

"Oh is that so?" Jane's eyes lid up as she said that. "But, how can he bring his paintings from England? I was mentioning to Eamon earlier, or was it you, Victoria, I can't remember who I said it to anyway, he has a room filled with art that has not sold. All of his art is great, thing is, all of his friends in York already have paintings he made, but he needs to have more clients," continued Jane.

Everyone thought for a moment, because yes, bringing art over from England was not going to be easy, they discussed what was to be done, when Eamon remembered he knew somebody quite well that ships things regularly between England and Ireland, he could call on him tomorrow and ask how to get the paintings over.

Drinks were served as they talked and then everyone went to bed, quite peacefully so, and the next day they all woke up with quite a lot to do. Eamon looked for his friend and arrange for the paintings to be brought over, Jane wrote to Heath and told him the news, and Dolly the art dealer took the carriage over to visit his friend. Dolly had room for Heath to show his art, but not for a few months, which was great, because that would be in the middle of spring anyway, plus the wedding could be postponed so far as Jane reckoned, she knew that Heath would rather show his art than go to his own wedding.

The next day Jane went with her cousin to Clongriffin to get rid of all the stones and rubble of what was once a castle. They woke up early and made it there before ten in the morning. It was a very windy day, very, very cold but Eamon and her had talked about clearing out as many rocks as possible before they would sell it.

Jane was standing in what used to be the entrance of the castle when she saw a door on the floor, one that neither she nor Eamon had ever seen before. Jane opened the door, which led to a basement. She did not have a torch to see where she was going but she reckoned so long as she left the door open she would be able to see where she was going.

The basement had several things from the seventeenth century, pieces of furniture, old candles, &c. She went to tell Eamon about it. He was beyond words. When he inherited the castle not a word had been mentioned about a basement. The place was very dusty, but since he was pulling rubble from other parts of the castle, he had a rag with him anyway, so he just started dusting everything.

"Look." He said "A letter" continued he. The letter read as such:

Dear owners of the castle:

I write to you on this day, June 1st on the day of our Lord 1693. I, Morgan of County Wicklow stayed in this castle last night. It needs be said that I was treated with scorn and violence. I, a traveler was tired and although I was offered rest the owners and staff called me a harlot and a wench. A pox on this house! I curse thee, whosoever might live or visit here from now until the end of days. The only way the curse will be broken or weakened is through love, I curse that word, love, wretched word. Finally, those without love, but yet with hatred I will come for their souls but not without tormenting them in this life first.

Morgan The Red of Wicklow

Both Jane and Eamon read the letter, they talked about what they read and came to the conclusion that it was she who cursed the place and she no doubt haunted many people that lived and visited here, but when Heath's great-great grandfather died it must have sufficed for her because most of the torments (though not all) stopped after his death. Neil was a very unhappy man who never knew that a witch had cursed him. When Neil died he was mourned even though he had been cruel with those around him and the seed of love was beginning to be planted. Later on Eamon (who had seen darkness) sought the light and found it with Heath who was a pure soul and with his cousin Jane.

There was still an enigma, though who caused the fire in the castle if there was nobody around? Was it Morgan's spirit, was she the cause of all this, or was it just an act of nature? The answer to that question will never be known, however, it is known for a fact that the fire did start in the grey room and it did spread quickly as well one should remember that nobody, not one living person, was in the castle then.

As evening settled Eamon and Jane went back to Dublin to Dolly's house where Victoria and he waited for them with some tea. During tea Eamon showed his friends the letter and asked their opinion on the matter. A lot was discussed, such as who was Morgan The Red and why had Heath's family been cruel to her. It was sadly concluded that nobody knew for sure who this witch was, however they knew that there was once a story of a woman who had once escaped life in Dublin and had gone to live in the mountains in Wicklow, far from everyone, and that she was believed to have been a witch that could curse people she did not like. Nobody believed in the story of the Wicklow witch and not one person knew for sure what her name had been however it was assumed that it was the same person.

Another subject that was talked about was that of Heath, Dolly had been in contact with him through a letter or two and had encouraged him to come at once and bring as much of his art as he could with him to Dublin.

Chapter 7

Heath came back to Ireland and just in time too. His paintings had shown up in boxes before he made it to Ireland which was easier, really. That way he did not have to carry them with him on his trip, so he had time to see how they had made it, and if they were damaged. Some had been but not tragically so. The paintings were sent by boat but a wind had picked up which caused the box that they had been placed in to move about, thus damaging a few of the paintings. Everything was fixed just in time. In art nothing is beyond repair. Invitations were sent to all the important people in Dublin, some as far as Galway, including Jane's parents and siblings. People came to see Heath's swiftly done paintings, and to have a drink and admire his work.

When it was time to give a toast to the artist, Heath said "Dearest Jane, without you this would never have happened, I am sad that we had to postpone the wedding, but I finally get to meet your family."

What went on in Jane's mind when they discussed the wedding was: First of all, a new life in York sounded nice, I mean let's face it, it wasn't Ireland and Jane loved Ireland, however she loved Heath, and could not imagine being away from him. Furthermore, she got along with his family quite well, so she knew that even though she would miss Galway tremendously, she would be able to visit from time to time, and she did, actually. She knew that she would miss the little things about her life in Galway, such as the way her mam's kitchen smelled when someone was cooking, or the cats that she had, she would miss them more than words could express, but she knew that life with a man as good as Heath would not be bad at all, because he was kind to her and his kindness and gentleness towards her would never stop, and she knew that more than anything in life, she wanted a man that would treat her right, so long as she lived. Jane was worried, though, because her parents saw the English as the conquerors that brought nothing but misery to Ireland and to see their daughter marry an Englishman was not what they had planned for her. A bit on that, though.

Jane's mother and father always dreamed that they would marry Jane to a hardworking Galway man and Jane met several of them, mostly older men that had made a good living for themselves in spite of the hardships in life. But she did not want any of those older, more mature men. She always wanted a youthful, sensitive, more artistic man and with Heath she got exactly what she wanted. Jane's parents, when they met Heath were sad that he was not exactly what they would have liked, but they could not deny the fact that Heath was tremendously kind and loving towards her so they talked in private with dearest Jane about what they were worried about, and she told them to stop worrying. But an Irish parent can never stop worrying and in time they grew to accept him as part of the family.

I will not spare you, my friends the ever so boring detail about the planning of the wedding since I already mentioned some things before, but there was one, detail you must know, which is that the wedding took place in Whitby Abbey one morning. It took ages to decide where to have the wedding. Some people suggested Fountains Abbey, others thought Castle Howard, while others reckoned York Minster would be a good idea. But after a long look at each place, Jane chose Whitby Abbey because that is where Heath proposed to her.

Jane looked stunning, as did brown eyed Heath, her in a white dress with white flowers and him in a blue suit. They did have a baby some time afterwards, named Daniel, and Eamon was the best of all uncles for him. Eamon provided everything that little Daniel needed, and showed him much love and affection.

Eamon had all of his furniture brought over from Ireland and settled a new life just across the street from Heath and Jane, where he visited baby Daniel every day, and told him stories about a haunted castle and of ghosts that once terrified the people that stayed there. Daniel, when he was no longer a baby, and could now comprehend everything, said that the stories must have been true, because he had a cat, and the cat would frequently stare at the wind and would get scared to death and hiss at it. Daniel was aware that there were many days when there was nobody there but the cat, and it would stare at nothingness as if something were moving, then the cat would run and hide in fear and hiss at the nothing. Cats are that way, though. They see things that we cannot see, such as beings from beyond the grave. Daniel's grey cat obviously saw spirits and was more than obviously terrified of them and would do anything possible to let Daniel know when a spirit would walk by. Since it was only a cat, it could only hiss and scratch, but that was enough to let Daniel know that something was in the room.

As for Victoria, Eamon had left her enough money for her to never need to work, and with that money she bought a small house in County Meath, where she attended her garden every day. Victoria did not need more than her garden in order to be entirely happy, and when she moved into her cottage with a large garden she was very, very happy.

Dolly kept in touch with Heath, and kept promoting his work, until in time he made Heath a very wealthy man. Heath did not become wealthy immediately, actually, you see he found that as time advanced and the nineteenth century came to a close and the twentieth century was born, the art world changed drastically, one day people in the art community wanted one thing, the next day it was out of style, and it was not always easy for tall, Dolly to find clients for Heath. But every year he found enough people interested in Heath's work that in time articles were being written about him in the papers, and such. Heath always had a dream, though, which was to show his work in places like Milan, Paris, etc, and in time, thanks to Dolly's help he did.

The End

POEMS

Exploring

When was the last time

That you went exploring,

What hill did you climb?

I expect it wasn't boring.

When was the last time

That you walked in the woods;

From the top could you climb
To unknown neighborhoods?

Have you learned something new,
Or re-discovered something old?
Did you have a clue?
You could be so bold?

Say, what did you learn?
That it snows in the desert,
And the arctic can burn,
Or you can get cut by a gentle fern.

Next time you are out
I ask you to observe
The hills and trees about
Nature is a teacher we deserve.

Kittens (a thought)

I wonder:

Do kittens have a soul?

Thing is, kittens cry, they smile, and kittens play too, they get angry, they get happy, they feel. I believe kittens do have a soul. Furthermore, regarding kittens, each one is different, so thus kittens must have a soul.

THE HOUSE

There is a small, brick house
On the road to a lake.
What beauty one can create,
Such a gorgeous house.

The place looks ancient, however
Were the owner's poor or rich,
Were they Davis, Williams, or Flinch?
Most gorgeous, small house ever.

I see chickens around it,

and a cow and two dogs.

They play in nearby bogs,

But the house is not lit.

Now you've heard of the house

Made out of brick,

Now empty and sick,

Who will buy this old house?

Will they repair it

Or will they tear it down?

Will they paint it orange, blue or brown?

No doubt a new light in here will be lit.

THE RIVER

There is a river,

don't you know,

It has a rainbow

of a rosy glow.

I took my shoes away

And wet my feet,

Felt my heart beet.

My feelings I did obey.

Listen to the song

the water makes

as a fall it makes

The drops fall long.

There is a river

And it flows just for us

You can hear it, thus,

it's sound can make you shiver.

Virgin Girl

Ode to thee oh virgin girl

Though you are so humble,

A God still came

from your womb.

I praise thee, Jewish, virgin girl.

You obeyed your heart and did not stumble.

It is because of your faith

We all have hope.

Old Man

How is life, old man,

Now that you are in heaven?

I hear a dove

singing in my ear.

If the dove sings, you are O.K.

You know, old man?

I heard your friends are angels.

I bet you tell them jokes.

I can see the angels laugh

Thank God you are at peace

And that you are able to

Make the angels laugh.

Cupid

Can a cupid wander through the fields of love,

wandering through gardens of hearts and of roses

and fly across the earth like a beautiful dove

to touch lovers with his arrows full of roses.

For sometimes love hits like a shock from up above.

When love strikes, we trust not our heads nor our noses.

So love brings happiness when life is indeed tough.

Love's strength is epic, like Hercules or Moses.

But love can break into countless of small pieces,

So be true to your heart and never let it go

even if you find yourself in awkward places

So always be gentle to your one and true love

whom as time flies by, you will love day by day

and never let go of that one whom you most love.

If love was not so... (a quick thought)

If love was not so TOUGH

If love was just a GAME

If love would not HARM

If love would not BURN

If love would not leave a SCAR

From Boy to Man

I

Once upon a time
A boy went for a walk
Without a dollar or a dime.

Beyond this world and time
Did our young boy walk,
Without speaking, like a mime.

II

Once our boy had left

His home, which was so new,

His family he as well left.

He went to conquer with no debt

Upon the rocks, mud and dew,

Going north, south, right and left.

III

The world was his,

And he was the world's

When he learned and saw bliss.

Only after learning, did the world become his

His arms, his face, his ears,

Everything now, with him is.

IV

Now our boy has grown into a man,

No longer a child is he

Proud is he of the life he ran,

And of how he became a man,

Of lessons life brought him,

From China, Iceland, to Iran.

During a Walk

I went for a walk today.

The sun was shining, the wind was calm.

There was a slight breeze, yet…

It bothered me not.

I believe it is a magic day

As if I was in the golden pot

At the rainbow's end;

So much peace to be got.

What's better than my sunny day,

Is the fact that I spot

Some bunnies at my foot's end.

"This must be a carrot," they thought.

A Thought

I wake up before dawn, people are still asleep. It will be a very busy day. I think of all the people in there beds, some of them barely climbing in them, yet my day has started...

I had a break around noon. Nobody to boss me around or tell me what to do, even if it's just for a little while. I'm off for a walk, and enjoy the day. I am not making e-mails or phone calls for just this peaceful moment. I will only look up to the trees and flowers, before the crazy day continues.

A Wet and Windy Day

Some people say

Cold weather brings gloom.

They hate the cold winds

Of one month, but love

The heat of May

I like a good windy day,

When the leaves of the trees

Move about like

Dancers prancing

Throughout the day.

When rain falls today

Upon the leaves

Flying through the air

I can not happier be,

Than upon that wet and windy day.

Happiness (a thought)

To me, happiness is not how much money you make in a day's work. Nor am I happy knowing what I own or what I can buy. No!

To me, happiness is waking up every morning to the song of a bird. I am also happy when I take a hot shower, and feel the drops on my body. As I walk I feel joy as I see a plant grow strong. A plant can be the greatest thing I see. Rain and sun is all a plant need to grow.

These are the joys I see in my life, not fancy cars or big bills, just simple things, like a plant or a tree. I think about the plants. Funny, as I shower in order to look and feel better, I I see the rain falling on the plants, and know that they too must feel better. I need the water, as does the plant.